# NEVER SAY DUKE

ERICA RIDLEY

ISBN: 1943794553
ISBN-13: 978-1943794553
Copyright © 2019 Erica Ridley
Model Photography © PeriodImages
Cover Design © Teresa Spreckelmeyer

**Rogues to Riches:**

Lord of Chance

Lord of Pleasure

Lord of Night

Lord of Temptation

Lord of Secrets

Lord of Vice

**Dukes of War:**

The Viscount's Tempting Minx

The Earl's Defiant Wallflower

The Captain's Bluestocking Mistress

The Major's Faux Fiancée

The Brigadier's Runaway Bride

The Pirate's Tempting Stowaway

The Duke's Accidental Wife

**The 12 Dukes of Christmas:**

Once Upon a Duke

Kiss of a Duke

Wish Upon a Duke

Never Say Duke

Dukes, Actually

The Duke's Bride

**Welcome to Christmas!**

Our picturesque village is nestled around Marlowe Castle, high atop the gorgeous mountain we call home. Cressmouth is best known for our year-round Yuletide cheer. Here, we're family.

The legend of our twelve dukes? Absolutely true! But perhaps not always in the way one might expect…

～

# CHAPTER 1

*T*heodore O'Hanlon, Major Viscount Ormondton, grimaced against the relentless pain. It pulsed through his head, his knee, his side. He promised himself the torture would soon end.

With a shaking finger, he cracked the curtains and allowed himself a brief glimpse outside the carriage.

Evergreens. Blinding sun on endless snow. A winding, narrow path up a remote mountain, leading him ever further from the ravages of war-torn France and the battles that still awaited him in London.

A bright red sign rose from the drifts of snow like a beacon:

*Welcome to Christmas!*

At last.

Theo closed the curtains tight. He was almost there.

He held no interest in the year-round Christmastide promised by the cozy little village. Nor did he care to be welcomed. Indeed, he had no wish to be recognized at all. That was why he was rattling along in a hired hack rather than the elegant coach-and-four bearing his family's crest.

It was also why he had come here straight from France, rather than wade into the whirling madness of London in full Season.

Theo desperately needed time to heal. A place to do so where no one would recognize him. A respite from all the chaos.

His childhood friend, the Duke of Azureford, had assured Theo the tiny village of Christmas was just the place. A winter wonderland in the northernmost corner of England, hundreds of miles from conflicts and battles. He was to avail himself of the duke's private cottage for as long as it took to regain his strength.

Theo prayed the process would not take long. He was so used to being active, being in control. Charging in from the front lines. He could not stand giving less than his all, in anything. Even if the reason for his diminished capacity was musket fire and the punishing hooves of his enemy's horse.

The carriage drew to a stop.

Theo's aching head sagged against the wall in relief. They had arrived at Azureford's secluded cottage. No more punishing journeys until his body could once again withstand the onslaught.

The young valet Theo had hired under an assumed name hopped out of the carriage in order to arrange the custom-built wheeled chair on the ground.

Theo hated the chair. He was not an invalid. He was a lord. An officer.

But the one time he'd allowed his pride to get the better of him in an attempt to rely solely on a pair of crutches and his own determination, Theo had buckled over, face first, right in front of a posting-house.

Never again.

An older gentleman with quick blue eyes and a shock of white hair cast a slow, impassive glance into the carriage's dark interior toward Theo.

That must be Swinton, Azureford's beloved butler. Theo carried a letter sealed with the duke's insignia for the staff to read, granting the letter's bearer all possible hospitalities.

The butler's gaze met his. "May I be of service, sir?"

Theo's lips might have curved if moving his facial muscles didn't feel like he was ripping the tender skin anew.

He had never been a "sir." He had been born a viscount, thanks to a courtesy title from his father. *Major* belonged to Theo alone. Both were inextricable from his identity. Yet for now, he was forced to hide the truth.

"Swinton, I presume?" Theo held out the folded letter. "I am sent by the Duke of Azureford."

The butler inspected the wax insignia before breaking the seal and reading the letter's contents.

Theo's blood chilled. Either Swinton was not a fast reader, or Azureford had included more information than expected.

His muscles tightened. Theo had come to this remote village in order to be anonymous. If the duke had destroyed that possibility, Theo would need to find alternate lodging. His stomach sank. He might not truly rest for another day or more.

Swinton handed the duke's letter to someone outside Theo's line of vision. "I shall have the maids air out the guest chambers. Do you require assistance into your chair?"

Theo clenched his jaw. How he hated any sensation of helplessness. He had not required assistance since he was a child, and rarely even then. He had pushed himself to new levels. Relied on no one's aid. *He* was the one sought after to help others. Counted upon to be strong, decisive, and capable in all things.

And, yes, he needed help into the accursed chair. Help, he bloody well was not going to ask for from his friend's butler.

Theo braced himself against a tidal wave of pain as he rose from the squab on his good leg and grappled for purchase on the frozen edge of the open doorway. He ducked his head as a gust of bitter wind threatened to rip the bandages from his face and expose the gashes bullets had left behind.

He could do this. Even if lowering himself into

that chair sapped the last bit of strength from his ravaged body, Theo would do it on his own.

Pain shot through his hip and side as he landed far too hard on the chair's leather surface. His swollen knee screamed with renewed pain as it jarred into place. The edges of Theo's vision blurred and went gray as he tried to block his body's panicked reaction and focus only on slowing his galloping heart.

He had done it. He was still capable. He was going to get better.

"What shall we call you?" The letter was back in the Butler's hands. "My master's instructions only refer to you as 'T.'"

"I..." Theo was concentrating too hard on masking his pain to dream up an appropriate pseudonym. "I don't need a name."

"Very well." Swinton gestured toward a footman. "Please see Mr. T to the guest chamber."

But the moment the footmen navigated the chair off the snow-packed lawn and inside the entryway, Theo held up a hand to still them. "I can follow from here."

Wheeling himself about had not been one of the many skills Theo had painstakingly prepared for before going off to war, but he had quickly learned its finer points. His arms had never been in better shape, and no longer tired from the effort.

It was the rest of his body that could not wait for the endless jostling and jarring to finally cease.

"This way." Swinton strode down the corridor

at a pace Theo very much appreciated. Brisk. Normal.

As if Theo was not a bandaged husk crumpled at all angles inside a wheeled chair, but a capable and healthy man.

The guest chamber was large and comfortably equipped, boasting several windows with a view of the snow-covered lane leading up to the majestic castle perched atop the mountain. This would do.

As soon as the rooms had been sufficiently aired, Theo would seal the curtains at once. Until he was completely healed, he could not be recognized. Not like this.

That was why he was so far from home. Why he had avoided inns and other such public meeting-houses. As far as the beau monde knew, he was still at war, leading his troops, doing his part.

"Shall I help you into the bed?" his valet asked with obvious hesitation.

Despite the wounds and bandages covering much of his face, Theo's infamous leveling glare had no trouble setting the lad aquiver.

"No," Theo growled. He tossed the lad a small pouch filled with coins. "Have Swinton divide this amongst the staff for their trouble. Then go have a rest. You deserve it."

When his valet quit the room, Theo glanced down at his twitching limbs and sighed. He was exhausted, but it would be some time before his brain and body were calm enough to sleep.

He had been prescribed laudanum but was loath to use it. For too many men, that way lay addiction. Theo would not allow himself to rely on anything but his own power.

His hands curled into fists. How he resented being plucked from the battlefield before the war was over. So many had been counting on him. His troops, his peers, the citizens whose rights he had been fighting for. As soon as Theo was better...

He reached into his inner pocket to retrieve a very different letter. This one had been addressed to him. Written by none other than Theo's soon-to-be betrothed, Lady Beatrice Munroe.

He wondered if his father had put her up to it.

Theo was but eight years old when Lady Beatrice had been born. That same day, their fathers determined that a mix of their bloodlines and associated political connections would be advantageous for all parties. Children were tools. This was how they could best be used.

The expectation to join two powerful families in marriage had been communicated to Theo at once, and to Lady Beatrice as soon as she was old enough to grasp her required role.

Until this winter, that had been the end of it. Theo had seen Lady Beatrice on occasion over the years, but they had not formed any particular attachment.

An attachment wasn't necessary.

Theo wasn't expected to enjoy Lady Beatrice's company. He was expected to marry her. Beget the requisite heir and a spare. Enhance the family's power and reach. Keep their sterling reputation polished.

To that end, one could not ask for a better

match than Lady Beatrice. Good breeding, good blood, good looks. Educated in all the proper things a Society wife was meant to master.

If anything, landing Lady Beatrice was a coup. Her father outranked his. And although Theo's future marquessate did not lack for coin, Lady Beatrice's dowry was eye-watering indeed.

What did it matter if he could not abide her personality?

He glared down at the letter in his hands. He did not need to unfold it for the tenth time to know what it said. This was a summons.

She dared to command him.

Their fathers had made their intentions known years before, but no contracts had been signed and Theo had made no promises.

Lady Beatrice felt it was time for that to change. Since her come-out three years earlier, she had quite enjoyed her reign among the other young ladies.

Theo preferred to make fewer waves. His unblemished reputation had kept him out of the caricatures and the society columns... until now. Apparently, his accomplishments at war had turned him into some sort of mystical hero.

Lady Beatrice had not missed his presence during her prior three Seasons. But now that his fame *in absentia* had eclipsed hers in person, his intended felt the time was ripe to make their betrothal official. She would become the toast of the *ton* overnight.

He wheeled himself closer to the fireplace in

order to toss Lady Beatrice's elegant penmanship into the crackling flames.

Theo had always known the chit was far more eager to reap the privilege that came with being a future marchioness than she was interested in him specifically.

Such pragmatism had never bothered him. He could not claim to feel differently, when they were both commodities. That was how *ton* marriages worked. He would marry her eventually, but Theo would be the one to decide when.

He had no intention of presenting himself next to the queen of the ball like some species of prized pet. Lady Beatrice might rule over other young ladies, but she would not rule him.

There was, however, one woman in London who Theo could be tempted to dance attendance upon.

This Season was his cousin Hester's come-out.

A painfully shy wallflower, Hester had long been terrified she would suffer through her entire Season without a single gentleman offering to stand up with her for a dance.

Theo glared at his useless leg. If anyone deserved to be the toast of the *ton*, it was Hester. The second he could dance again, he would ensure his name appeared on every one of her dance cards. He'd encourage his unmarried friends to follow suit until every man present realized just how special Hester was.

She needn't worry. Theo would save the day. He just... needed a little time to heal.

Movement outside the open windows caused

Theo to drag his gaze from the dancing orange flames out to the gently falling snow.

A young lady walked alone down the winding narrow path from the castle, accompanied only by a coal black cat with a tall plume of a tail, his paws obscured by snow.

Theo's curiosity turned to growing disbelief as he watched the cat accompany its mistress like a dog. The beast hurried to her side after falling behind to sniff something. Glanced over his shoulder to ensure her impending arrival if it happened to prance too far ahead. Paused when she paused, continued when she continued. Theo watched, transfixed.

The closer the pair drew to Azureford's cottage, the more details he could pick out.

The woman's hair was the red-brown of autumn leaves. Her lips and cheeks were a flushed, becoming pink. Her coat was the same dark green as the snow-speckled forest behind her, her boots as dark black as the cat's fur.

She was too old to be a debutante, too young to be on the shelf. Her attire appeared warm, serviceable, and well-tailored, but without any particular pretension toward current fashions.

In other words, the mystery lady was of indeterminate age, indeterminate background, indeterminate *everything*.

Theo could not help but be intrigued.

Almost without fail, every person he came in contact with all but broadcast who and what they were. Not this woman. Even her cat made no bloody sense.

As he watched, she spied something in the trees just across the street from his window.

Without bothering to so much as glance over her shoulder to make eye contact with her pet, the woman held up a gloved palm and murmured, "*Heel!*" as if the ball of black fluff at her side actually was a dog.

Despite the pain, Theo could not help but indulge a small quirk of his lips at such folly. Obviously, a cat would never obey a command like—

His jaw fell open as the beast practically rolled its feline eyes in reluctant submission and sat on its haunches. How on earth…?

The woman paid no attention to her improbably obedient pet, as though she took it as a matter of course that all cats should respond without question to their masters' commands.

Instead, she scrambled over the hill of snow lining the road. With a tender look upon her face, she, too, dropped to her haunches and disappeared completely out of sight.

Rapt, Theo rolled his chair closer to the window.

Moments later, the woman rose to her feet with aching slowness, her leather gloves cupped together to protect a tiny puff of feathers. A baby bird. She tilted her head back and craned her face up toward the branches overhead. Theo's heart skipped in trepidation.

She would not attempt to climb a tree. She *would not* attempt to climb a tree.

She was absolutely going to climb the tree.

# CHAPTER 2

*M*iss Virginia Underwood and "Duke," her cherished cat and faithful companion, were strolling through Christmas on their afternoon constitutional when Virginia spied the tiny orange feet of a baby redwing poking up from a snowbank.

Oldest friend or not, Duke was first and foremost a cat, and a proficient one at that. Which meant he was quite adept at pouncing upon anything that resembled prey. Under normal circumstances, Virginia allowed—nay, *encouraged*—her cat to behave as catlike as he pleased. She did not believe any living thing should be prevented from the pursuit of happiness.

Except in the case of animals in need. Hurt creatures deserved to be helped.

Ever since she'd come to Christmas, Virginia had been unable to resist adopting strays and nursing wounded beasts back to health. Once her beloved patients were released back into the wild... well, nature could do whatever nature would do. But for as long as she was in control, baby birds like this one would be free to live another day.

After depositing the chick back into its nest, Virginia dropped down from the tree and brushed the debris from her gloves and person as best she could.

Her bonnet had gone askew and her freshly pressed coat was wrinkled, but what did it matter? Christmas was the furthest haven in England from the disapproving glares of beau monde grand dames and other such exacting personages. Just like her cat, here Virginia was free to be as Virginia-like as she pleased.

Unlike her cat, Virginia had not suddenly disappeared.

"*Duke*," she whispered.

He did not respond.

"*Duke*," she called a little louder.

Nothing.

She sent a suspicious glance up the tree. No sign of Duke there, either. Nor did his paw-prints lead in this direction.

In fact, it appeared as though he had set off in the direction of... the Duke of Azureford's cottage. Every one of the wide glass windows were inexplicably cranked open, despite the falling snow and winter chill.

Just as Virginia could not resist adopting strays, her cat could not resist the temptation of a beckoning window.

She dashed across the street. Little paw-prints in the snow led past the appropriately closed front door to just below the sill of a ridiculously gaping window. There the trail stopped.

The naughty beast had invited himself inside.

With a sigh, Virginia presented herself at the main door. She did her best to summon a winning smile when the butler answered her knock.

Swinton neither smiled nor frowned at discovering her upon the front step. "Good afternoon, Miss Underwood. How may I be of service?"

Virginia's smile fell. It probably wasn't doing her any favors. The back of her neck heated in response to the confession she was about to make.

"You have an unexpected visitor," she admitted.

"How do you know?"

"I followed his tracks." She motioned around the corner. "I think he went through that window."

Swinton blinked. "He left through the window?"

"Entered," she corrected. "He might be plump for a cat, but he has no trouble leaping to great heights when he puts his mind to it."

"Your *cat* went through the window?"

She nodded. "May I fetch him?"

Swinton did not immediately respond. Worse, he maintained that same frustrating mask of no-smile, no-frown.

Those were the two expressions Virginia could reliably read. Without one or the other to guide her, she often did not know how to proceed.

Like now. Did Swinton not understand her query? Should she impress upon him the importance of corralling her runaway cat before Duke took it upon himself to frolic in the larder, or disrupt the crystal on the table, or leap at the sparkling glass of the chandeliers?

Or had she missed some other cue? Should she have begun with a more effusive greeting? Or a more abject apology? Or—blast, this was probably it—inquired whether the Duke of Azureford was at home and receiving visitors?

Swinton stepped aside. "Of course, you must retrieve your cat. Shall I summon a few footmen to aid you?"

She shook her head. "Even the most fearless hunter will hide when he senses he has become the prey."

"As you say." Swinton ushered her inside and shut the door behind her. "May I take your coat and bonnet?"

"I shall only be a moment." She hurried forward in search of her cat.

Duke was not in either of the front parlors, which were the only rooms Virginia had spent time in on previous occasions. Nor was Duke in the kitchen or the larder, to Virginia's great relief. The dining room was also intact.

She headed toward the living quarters at the rear of the cottage, grateful that Azureford was not present to witness this gross trespass of his home.

"*Duke,*" she called into each open doorway she passed. "Duke, please come out."

Not that she could blame him for running off when opportunity had presented itself. It was one of the reasons they shared such a kinship. Virginia had often wished she could dive into someone else's life, too.

*"Duke..."* She nudged open a cracked door and came to a full stop.

There, perched high atop a wardrobe with his dark shoulders hunched low and his furry hips wriggling high, Duke prepared to pounce.

Just below, seated in a stiff, wheeled chair beside a four-poster bed, sat a man cloaked half in bandages and half in shadow.

His face snapped toward hers. *"Get out."*

She stepped closer. "I've come for my cat."

"I don't have your cat," the man growled.

"He who does not look, knows not what he possesses." She rushed forward to place herself between the innocent bystander and her mischievous cat before Duke could cause the poor man more harm than he'd obviously suffered.

He flinched at her sudden movement, then gave an almost simultaneous wince, as if the mere act of flinching had caused him extraordinary pain.

Virginia's heart twisted. She might not be competent at reading expressions or subtle social cues but *wincing* and *flinching* were behaviors she very much recognized. Every single one of her wounded strays had begun just so before they healed.

"Don't take another step," the man ordered, his harsh voice little more than a cold rasp.

She inched closer.

Normally, Virginia did her best to follow all explicitly spoken directives.

If anything, she often wished everyone could state their desires plainly, instead of expecting the crease of a brow or the position of a painted fan to convey what actual words could communicate so much more effectively.

Wounded strays were different. They didn't *want* her help. They *needed* her help. They just didn't know it yet.

"Don't move," she whispered. "I'll do my best to block the attack, but he is very good at being a cat."

The bandaged man went completely immobile. It was as if he was cloaked not just in dappled shadow and strips of cloth but encased in a thick layer of ice. His long black lashes did not blink. His wide lips did not grimace. Not even a twitch on the visible half of his chiseled face.

With effort, she tore her gaze from his soft black hair and rigid muscles and spun to glare at the fluffy predator atop the wardrobe.

She held out her arms. "Come here, right now."

Ignoring her, Duke lowered his haunches and bared his teeth.

"I mean it." Virginia lifted her hands higher. "Right now, Duke."

He gave a loud hiss, retracted his claws, and launched himself into her arms.

She cuddled him to her chest. "You naughty scamp. Please leave nice gentlemen alone. You could have hurt…" She turned toward the bandaged man. "What was your name?"

"I didn't give it." His voice was as frigid as the wind outside.

Virginia liked the cold. She sat on the edge of a wingback chair, careful to keep Duke trapped in her arms. "I apologize for my cat's behavior. I didn't mean for him to stalk you. He slipped away while I was climbing a tree and…"

She clamped her teeth together. *Short explanations.* That was one of the rules. *One cannot say the wrong thing when one says nothing at all.* That had been the very first rule. She was breaking them both.

The man stared at her. No smile, no frown. No mockery. He was a mystery.

She gazed back in interest. If he was this handsome half-hidden in bandages, he must be absolutely stunning when fully unveiled. She gave Duke an extra scratch behind the ears. Coming here had been an excellent choice.

"Shouldn't you be somewhere else?" the man said at last.

She shook her head. "We're on our afternoon constitutional. The castle won't have supper for a few more hours."

His eyes narrowed. "You're a guest in the castle?"

"No." That answer was easy to keep short. Virginia knew better than to say too much about herself.

The man glanced at the open bedchamber door, then back to her. "Where is your maid?"

"Though the sloth traverses its path alone, peace is all around it." She, too, cast her concerned gaze about the otherwise empty chamber. "Where is your nurse?"

18

"I do not have one," the man enunciated in harsh, clipped syllables.

Perfect.

He needed Virginia.

She rose to her feet. "I'll be back tomorrow."

"Do not come back tomorrow." His dark eyes glittered with the fire's reflection. "Do not come back at all."

Virginia tilted her head. The Duke of Azureford had personally told her she was welcome back at any time.

This man was clearly not the Duke of Azureford.

Therefore, she would ignore his bluster, just as she would with any creature too scared to trust a stranger. She would prove her goodwill with action.

"I'll be your nurse," she promised him. "Don't worry."

"I don't require a nurse," he said, his voice and posture stiff. "I want for nothing at all."

This could not be true. "Nothing?"

"Perhaps a spare face," he said, his tone harsh. "And my favorite ice cream. And a new leg. Is there a 'spare leg vendor' in this village?"

"I'll do what I can," she assured him. He would be a pleasure to visit. She was already more intrigued than she dared admit.

He stared at her for a long moment. "Who *are* you?"

"Virginia," she answered, and whisked Duke out of the bedchamber and away from temptation.

# CHAPTER 3

*T*he following afternoon, Theo unwound his bandages. He turned to face the looking-glass with determination. The ragged welts crisscrossing half his face glared back at him.

Was he a monster? Perhaps. But he was not a monster on the brink of death, and for that he was grateful. His wounds looked raw and swollen, but not gangrenous. His face would scar. His side would heal. His knee... Well, at least Theo got to keep his leg.

Gently, he reapplied fresh bandages. Not so much to protect the new skin, as to hide the unsightly mess from view.

The damage was not as severe as he had at first feared when he'd regained consciousness in the middle of a bloody battlefield. He would need to take care not to reopen the freshly healed wounds as he worked on regaining his strength.

A footman entered the guest chamber with a portable writing desk under one arm. "Where shall I place this, sir?"

"I'll take it." Theo rolled forward and held out a hand.

By necessity, he had arrived with little. Only the possessions he'd had with him in France. Toiletries, regimentals, a book of poetry, Lady Beatrice's letter.

He had not yet written a response. Indeed, until this letter, he and Lady Beatrice had never corresponded at all.

Perhaps it was unromantic of him to have tossed his future wife's first communiqué into the fire.

Not that she had written a love letter. In addition to demanding he present himself at once in order to increase her popularity by making her a "war hero's" intended bride, Lady Beatrice had presumed to dictate where, when, and how.

Apparently, the fête of the Season was to take place in two months' time. Everyone of importance would be there, and that number needed to include Theo. Lady Beatrice expected him to stand up with her in a dance not once, not twice, but thrice. Eyebrows would raise. People would whisper. And then they would announce the betrothal to gasps and applause so that Lady Beatrice would see her name in the Society papers, linked to his.

Of course, he would not submit to such machinations. He had no wish to be gossiped about, and even less intention of allowing his future bride to preside over him like a puppet-master. Theo obeyed no one's orders but his superior officers' and his own.

He opened the lid of the writing desk to examine its contents. Quills, ink, foolscap, a small cloth, a bit of sand. Everything one might require, if one had a message to dispatch. Unfortunately, he had no good news to impart, such as when his legs would walk again.

Theo removed the writing table from his lap and placed it on the tea table. There was no sense penning unnecessary correspondence. He would write Lady Beatrice as soon as he could estimate a date for his return to London. For now, it was better for her to continue to imagine her "dashing war hero" off slaying enemies in France than rolling himself about in a wheeled chair because he was not strong enough to do aught else.

He glanced down at his leg. As soon as it could support him again, he would return to London and make a formal offer. Not in a ballroom, but to Lady Beatrice's father. She would be appeased, and more importantly, so would Theo's sire.

Theo's lips twisted. Wedding the woman Father had chosen for him could be the missing piece to finally earn the marquess's approval.

Or at least a modicum of recognition.

He slid a glance over at the writing desk. Theo supposed if he sent word to anyone, it ought to be his parents. His stomach tightened. He could already imagine Father's familiar disappointment in his sole offspring. He had been furious when Theo went off to war. That he got himself injured would only serve to enrage the marquess further.

For Father, oppressed, impoverished, or terror-stricken people were irrelevant. Especially those in foreign lands. All that mattered was the title. Which meant marrying well, bearing sons, and avoiding risking one's neck in battle if one was the heir apparent to a marquessate. Did Theo *want* the title to go to some beggarly cousin? Where were his priorities?

To some degree, Theo had wanted to get his hands on the marquessate his entire life. Not as a sudden inheritance after his father's death, but as an opportunity to manage at least some small part of it side-by-side with his father while the marquess still lived.

Theo had studied every journal of accounts endless times. Visited every inch of property they owned. Interviewed every tenant, every member of staff, to understand their roles and needs and abilities. Researched areas to improve, places to invest, opportunities for growth. By now, Theo knew the marquessate even better than the worn book of poetry that never left his side.

None of it mattered.

Father had never once inquired about Theo's opinion about any matter. He certainly had no interest in sharing an inch of control. It was perhaps one of the reasons Theo had gone off to war despite the risks. At home, he had no duties. He was useless.

Theo wished to be *useful*. To be needed. To matter.

Not decades hence, when he inherited the title and its accompanying position in the House of Lords. But today. Now. While he was young and strong and capable. Or had been.

He was still young, at least, Theo reminded

himself as his swollen knee throbbed and the fresh scars beneath his bandages hurt like the devil. He might not be strong or useful at this precise moment, but he would not rest until his body fully recovered.

How long would that take? Would he be stuck in this village for weeks? Months?

Theo rolled over to the window and slid his finger in the crack between the curtains. He gazed outside at the relentlessly beautiful view. Anyone could fall in love with a place like this. It wasn't too far from his own country pile. Theo's problem wasn't the town of Christmas. His problem was—

A familiar figure picked her way down the snow-packed lane. Today, Virginia was cloaked in a coat of berry red. In one gloved hand hung a large wicker basket. The black cat was nowhere to be seen.

Theo let the curtain fall. No doubt the beast was imprisoned inside the basket. An intelligent precaution, but unnecessary. All the windows were closed tight today. Neither she nor her cat would be coming inside.

The faint thud of a knock sounded from the other side of the cottage.

Theo wheeled as fast as he could to throw open his chamber door and growled into the empty corridor, "I am not at home!"

Scant moments later, the butler appeared with a calling card in his hands. "You have a guest."

"I am not receiving," Theo enunciated.

"I'll add her card to the dish in the front parlor." Swinton paused. "Shall I show her in there or do you prefer visitors here in your private drawing room?"

Theo clenched his jaw. "Neither. Please relay to Virginia—"

"Miss Underwood." Swinton's diction was clipped, and his expression detached, but the rebuke was clear.

Theo stared back at him. He had never been interrupted by a butler, or a servant of any kind, much less reprimanded by one.

He reminded himself that Swinton was unaware of Theo's rank. For all the butler knew, "Mr. T" could be a street sweeper or a boxing-master or a common cutpurse. Nonetheless, he had arrived bearing a promise of hospitality sealed by the duke's own signet. Swinton ought to behave accordingly.

Theo forced himself to reply in cold, even tones. "I did not know her name was Miss Underwood."

"Now you do." The butler's lack of expression indicated Theo was the one wasting his time. "Front parlor or guest parlor?"

Theo unleashed his infamous quelling glare. No one had ever withstood its devastating effect without cowering in its wake.

Swinton practically yawned.

Theo gritted his teeth. Bloody bandages. A man could not unleash a proper glare when trussed up like an Egyptian mummy.

"Look here," Theo said. "Did your master not give you explicit instructions on how to extend hospitality to a houseguest?"

"He did, indeed." Swinton pulled the folded letter from an inner pocket and handed it back to Theo. "Look here."

Theo read the letter in disbelief.

As promised, Azureford had respected Theo's wish for anonymity. He was indeed granted the run of the cottage and referred to only as T. That was the first sentence of several paragraphs.

The rest of the contents recounted Theo's "surly disposition," "tendency toward reclusive behavior," and "devil's own stubbornness."

The final lines humorously implored the staff not to allow Theo to "get away with too much" and for Swinton in particular to treat their houseguest exactly as he would treat Azureford himself. The duke no doubt had enjoyed a hearty laugh as he penned his instructions.

Sourly, Theo handed the letter back to the butler.

Swinton's expression did not change, but his eyes hinted at the humor he no doubt found in their circumstance. "Following my master's orders to the letter, sir."

Theo gave a thin smile. "Can you please inform Miss Underwood—"

Virginia rushed around the corner and into the corridor, the wicker basket clutched in her hands.

"There you are." She dug inside the basket and handed him a spoon. "If you don't eat quick, it's all going to melt."

Theo accepted the spoon out of reflex. "All what will melt?"

"Your favorite ice cream, as requested." She

swept past him into the guest parlor, relocated the writing desk from the tea table to the floor, and began unpacking the contents of her basket.

Theo wheeled over to her as quickly as he could. "What do you think you're doing?"

"What I can. You must know a surgeon cannot replace your head, nor does Christmas offer limb exchanges." She placed dish after dish atop the table. "You did not mention which flavor of ice cream was your favorite, so I asked the castle kitchen to make every choice they could think of."

Theo stared at the growing selection of ice cream, swung his gaze up to her, then back to the ice cream. He hadn't expected Virginia to interpret sarcasm as an actual suggestion. Or to return for another visit at all.

But she had, and the tea table looked delicious. His stomach growled in appreciation. It was nigh impossible to maintain a haughty attitude to someone who arrived bearing every flavor of ice cream.

"How many spoons did you bring?" Theo said gruffly. He was not going to eat all this without her.

"One." Virginia pointed encouragingly. "It's in your hand."

Theo knew where *his* spoon was. He glanced over his shoulder, where he fully expected the gloating butler to be blatantly eavesdropping on the conversation.

He was not disappointed.

"At once, sir." Swinton disappeared to fetch a second spoon.

Virginia stared at the untouched dishes of ice cream. "You're not eating."

"I'm waiting for your spoon to arrive."

"I see." Her gaze slid to the empty basket. "I should have brought more."

"You displayed extraordinary resourcefulness," he said firmly. He could not let her think he had found fault with such a selfless gift.

She did not lift her eyes to his.

He wished she would.

Yesterday, Theo had been desperate to chase her out of his guest chamber. He did not want anyone to see him like this. Not even some mystery beauty who climbed trees and owned an attack cat.

All night long, he had wished he had taken a closer look. He could recall every wave of her red-brown tendrils, the angle of her cheekbones, the dusky rose of her lips, but he had not managed to register the color of her eyes.

He had believed this hole in his memory was due to the lack of candles in his chamber. Theo had no desire for anyone else to gaze upon his injuries, and even less wish to brood over them himself. The only light came from the flickering flames of the fire.

But perhaps the shadowed interior was not completely at fault. Virginia was right in front of him. Just on the other side of the tea table. And her eyes had not met his even once.

Swinton stalked into the room. "A spoon for the lady."

Virginia's gaze briefly met Swinton's as she accepted the spoon. "Thank you."

He did not excuse himself.

Theo slid him an impatient glance. He had no wish to be unchaperoned with any marriageable young lady, but nor did he need the butler literally looming over their shoulders.

Swinton cleared his throat in submission. "I will instruct a footman to be on call in the doorway."

Although the butler left with obvious reluctance, Theo suspected Swinton's interests lay less in maintaining propriety than witnessing whatever surprises Virginia would unveil next.

He wheeled closer. "Now we're ready."

She pointed at the ice cream with her spoon. "Which one is your favorite flavor?"

"I don't have one," he admitted. "I like all ice cream."

"Then I did bring the right ones." Her gaze briefly met his in triumph.

*Green*. His breath caught. Her eyes were a brilliant, unblemished green. Lighter than jade or emerald or the forest green pelisse she had been wearing the day before. A brilliant, crystal green. As beautiful as the sea sparkling beneath the sun.

"Eat," she commanded. "He who waits for the moon to come to him wastes the night without having traveled an inch."

Theo prided himself on not obeying any chit's authoritative commands, no matter how poetic. But perhaps just this once…

"You, too," he commanded as authoritatively as

a half-mummified lord with a smear of ice cream on his upper lip could. "Before it melts."

They passed the sweet, creamy dishes in surprisingly companionable silence. Just two people, unabashedly more interested in devouring a cornucopia of flavors than wasting time with conversation. She was the strangest woman he had ever met, and oddly refreshing. He was surprised how much he liked her unpredictability.

"I do not require a nurse," he informed her after the last drop of ice cream was gone.

He expected his stern words to ruin the moment. That was why he had uttered them.

"You think you don't," Virginia agreed as she stacked the empty dishes back inside her basket. "You'll see."

He stared at her in disbelief. Had the daft woman truly just implied she knew his mind better than he did himself?

"See here," he began.

She jerked her head in his direction at once. "You are absolutely right. I should change your bandages."

He blinked. "I just changed my bandages."

"And now you've smudges of strawberry and chocolate on them." She rose to her feet and glanced about the room. "Where are your clean cloths?"

Theo didn't answer. He didn't have to. Virginia was already washing her hands in the basin, which was conveniently located right next to his supply of clean bandages.

She brought them over to his chair and knelt at

his feet. "I apologize in advance if this hurts you. It is important to keep wounds clean."

"It won't hurt."

He clenched his teeth and braced himself for the pain, and the horror that would contort her pretty face the moment she saw the damage that lay beneath.

She cupped a soft, warm hand to the good side of his face as she slowly unwrapped the bandages from the other.

Theo's wounds did not hurt. Not yet. But he had no doubt he would flinch the same moment she did.

The pad of her thumb brushed lightly against his good cheek as she removed the last bandage. "You look splendid."

"You mean my wounds look splendid?" he stammered.

"I mean you." She did not lower her palm from his cheek. "When you were bandaged, I believed you were the most handsome man I had ever seen. Now I know without a doubt."

His chest thumped in confusion. That was an extremely flattering and extremely forward statement to make. Yet she had delivered her judgment with complete matter-of-factness, as if his beastly handsomeness despite his scars was a fact universally acknowledged and not a quirk native solely to her.

She lifted her hand from his face and folded her fingers in her lap.

He felt the loss to his bones.

"Aren't you going to redress my wounds, Nurse?" he growled.

He did not know why he was snarling at her. He did not want her help. Theo could dress his wounds himself and most likely would have to fix whatever she did. The problem was that she had been touching him, and now she was not. It made him feel even more beastly than when covered in strips of cloth.

"You don't need bandages," she said. "You've new skin now. It ought to breathe. One must keep it clean and dry, but there is no reason to keep it hidden."

He arched his brows. "Other than the disfigurement and raw flesh?"

"Bah." She carried the untouched roll of bandages back to the side table. "Duke has come home with worse."

He gazed at her.

"Duke, my cat," she explained quickly. "Not Azureford."

He cleared his throat. "I imagined."

Her lips curved. "That's how Duke and I met. He lost a fight with a much bigger cat and I had to sew him back up from groin to sternum. We've been inseparable ever since."

"That's… one way to bond," Theo managed.

She gave him an awkward pat on his shoulder. "Don't worry. I have years of experience with strays."

"I am not a stray," he spluttered. "I am—"

Viscount Ormondton. An Army Major.

A man desperate to cling to anonymity and privacy for as long as he could.

He hiccupped.

Damn it. He clenched his teeth and pressed his lips tight to try to hide the spasms.

The next hiccup nearly bounced him out of his seat.

Her expression gentled. "Would you like a cup of water?"

Theo glared at her. He had developed his infamous cutting glance specifically because sometimes when emotion got the best of him, so did the hiccups. He could not always trust his mouth to respond as he wished. But his eyes... Those were always more than capable of slaying their victims with a single glance. He turned their full force on Virginia.

She patted his shoulder. "I'll get you some water."

The moment she left his line of sight, he closed his eyes and willed his hiccups to cease using the only trick that had ever worked. Holding his breath, he recited his favorite poem in his head. Either the hiccups would go away, or he would pass out.

Anything was better than having a slip of a girl pat him on the shoulder as if he were a child in leading strings.

When Virginia returned with the water, Theo's hiccups were gone. He gave her his haughtiest glare, as if to say a lord of his stature could not fathom why anyone would think him in need of a cup of water.

She thrust it into his hand anyway.

As she took her seat across from him, she motioned toward his ruined knee. "Let me see your leg."

"No." He nearly crushed the cup of water in his hand, so swift and adamant was his response.

"I can see that it is swollen. Is the wound internal, external, or both?"

He glared at her. "Internal."

His leg had taken a horse hoof right to the kneecap. The fractures had fused back together, but not in all the right places. It was not the kind of break that could be reset. And he definitely did not want anyone looking at it.

"Clearly you can bend your knee," she said as she considered him. "Can you straighten it?"

"Yes." Any time he wished to pass out from pain, all he had to do was straighten his leg. Come to think of it, it wouldn't be a half-bad cure for hiccups.

"Can you put weight on it?"

"Not for long," he hedged. Not even a full second. Bullets to the cheek hadn't felled him as quickly as his knee now could.

She reached toward it.

He nearly jumped out of his skin.

She patted his other knee. "Shh. I won't hurt you. Let me feel."

Theo concentrated on not losing the edges of his vision as she pressed her gentle hands to the swollen lump of his knee.

"Are you taking laudanum?" she asked.

"No," he gritted out.

She frowned. "You are a very strange man."

"You are a very strange woman," he retorted. There. Now he'd proven he had a face to rival Medusa and the clever repartee of an eight-year-old lad.

"You need crutches," Virginia announced.

"I have crutches."

"How often do you practice with them?"

"I don't need them." He pointed at his knee. "I'm staying right here until this is back to normal."

"It won't heal properly if you don't exercise it."

"It will heal faster if I leave it alone."

She paused. "How many times has this happened to you?"

He stared at her. "This is the first and only time it shall ever happen to me."

"Then I have more experience." She lifted her chin with confidence. "Tomorrow we will start with small stretches and work our way up. The secret is not to add pressure before you are ready, but to keep the muscle supple and limber."

He gazed doubtfully at his ruined knee. "More likely, I'll never walk again, and you don't want to tell me."

She lifted a shoulder as if him walking or not was as inconsequential as the falling snow. "You definitely won't if you don't try."

He scoffed. "And you are the only one who can fix me?"

"No one can fix you," she said matter-of-factly.

He waited for the rest.

She said nothing more.

"Not the most inspiring of speeches," he said dryly.

"You already know I can help you. I told you yesterday." Virginia inclined her head. "You needn't worry. Now you have me."

Nothing could worry him more.

Theo folded his arms over his chest. "You intend to spend your holiday playing nurse to a stranger?"

"I'm not a tourist," she said. "I live in the castle. We'll work on your recovery every day for as long as you need me."

He frowned. "You live in the castle?"

She nodded. "Many people do."

"I assumed just servants," he admitted. "And the Marlowe family, of course."

"When Mr. Marlowe died, he bequeathed the castle to the villagers." Her green eyes shone with gratitude. "I was already living there. So was my friend Noelle, and many others."

Perhaps this was a stroke of luck.

Theo slid his gaze toward the writing desk lying forgotten beneath the tea table. He had been hesitant to write to his father. In part, because he had no eagerness to receive the imminent haranguing, but also because he did not want Azureford's staff to deduce Theo's identity from the address on the letter.

Virginia changed all that. If the letter included no return direction and was smuggled into the castle's outgoing correspondence by way of his self-appointed nurse, no one need be the wiser.

The wild card in the plan was Virginia.

Would she follow his instructions? He suspected she would. She seemed eager to help. Would she recognize his father's name? He suspected she would not. She lived in the furthest possible point from London Society. She had no reason to memorize lineages of the peerage.

But it was still a risk. He would have to decide whether to trust her.

"No crutches," was all he said aloud. No crutches in front of her, anyway. He preferred his facial contortions and grunts of pain to stay private.

"Not yet," she agreed. "Put ice or snow on your knee once an hour. Tomorrow we'll start the exercises."

With that, she picked up her basket and was gone.

# CHAPTER 4

*V*irginia turned to her cat. *"Heel."*

Duke sent her a sullen glance but settled outside the aviary to wait for her as he did every morning.

He was not angry at her for refusing him entrance to a buffet full of birds. He was miffed at having been disinvited to yesterday's constitutional.

"Maybe this afternoon," she promised him, and slipped inside the aviary.

He knew as well as Virginia did that she would not be able to leave him behind for long. She loved him too much. They understood each other. Virginia never asked Duke to be anything but what he was or do anything but what he did.

In return, Duke kept coming back because he liked her just as she was, too.

She fished in her reticule for a bag of seed and began tossing the treats about the aviary. After having sat in half-finished construction for years, the aviary had finally opened three months prior.

On its first day, it contained a single partridge. One month later, Virginia had taken it upon herself to donate one of her own rescues she'd recently rehabilitated.

Although she had doubled the population with a single gift, a two-bird aviary did not attract many guests. In fact, after the opening celebration, Virginia was the only resident who bothered to return. She was here so often it almost functioned like her private nook.

Virginia had been using a pair of abandoned outbuildings near the castle as temporary shelters for the various strays she had helped over the years. One was for birds, the other for any animal she dared not leave alone in an enclosed structure full of wounded birds.

Last month, she had decided it was silly to tend both to overcrowded outbuildings and an underpopulated aviary. One by one, she smuggled each of her rescued birds from her secret sanatorium into the castle aviary.

No one had noticed.

Virginia didn't care. She wasn't tending strays for tourists' sakes. She was saving tiny lives.

"Dasher," she called softly as she wound her way through the aviary's greenery. *Aha.* There he was.

The chaffinch had hurt its wing when it had crashed into her friend Penelope's chimney. In the weeks since Virginia had rescued him, his wing had healed, and he could once again fly. The latest in a long line of successes.

She hugged herself as she gazed about the

aviary. It was now her second home, but it hadn't begun that way. When Virginia had first arrived in Christmas, she had been skittish around animals of all kinds. The loud squawks and sudden flaps of wings startled her.

Learning not to flinch had been the first project she had given herself. Little by little, she lost her fear and learned to love animals instead. Now they were her family.

With a creak, the door to the aviary swung open.

Virginia looked over in surprise. Occasionally one of her friends would seek her out, but the man who had just entered was the solicitor handling Mr. Marlowe's estate.

She glanced away.

"Good morning, Miss Underwood." He stepped further into the aviary and scribbled something in a small notebook. "I didn't expect anyone to be here."

"One need not expect the sun for it to rise every morn," she mumbled.

"You will be pleased to know that we are almost ready to move forward with Mr. Marlowe's final plans for the aviary."

Virginia was not pleased to know. The plans did not include Virginia at all.

"When?" she asked.

The solicitor smiled at her. "I'll let you know."

She did not understand his smile. The loss of her sanctuary was not good news, but a disaster for her and her rescues. They were used to the aviary now. She did not want to return to using a tiny outbuilding.

"May I keep the aviary?" she asked hesitantly.

"I'm afraid not." Now the solicitor was frowning. "It is not meant for your personal use, but to realize the dreams of our town's founder."

Virginia nodded her understanding. A frown was appropriate. Her stomach felt as though it were tumbling over a cliff.

It was happening again. As soon as she found something she liked, somewhere she felt loved, she was pushed out. Virginia's presence could be tolerated in short bursts, but not for long. She should know by now.

Her own parents had barred her from the schoolroom. Then polite company. Then their home. They had driven her to an asylum for problematic young ladies and never returned.

"Are you all right?" the solicitor asked, stepping closer.

She jerked away before he could touch her. Even though it was not his fault, he was ruining one of the few things she had come to think of as her own. A place she belonged. Somewhere she could be useful. She adopted her strays because she knew what it was like not to be wanted.

Virginia quit the aviary without asking further questions. Soon it would no longer be available to her. What more did she need to know?

She would not focus on the loss. The birds were not the only ones who needed her. For the first time, she had an opportunity to be useful to another person.

Duke meowed as she stepped out of the aviary.

"You're right. We still have each other." She scooped him into her arms and fetched a basket to transport him in. "We'll visit Mr. T together."

When Swinton answered the door, Virginia presented her calling card and remembered to inquire about the Duke of Azureford before asking to see her patient.

Swinton personally escorted her down the corridor to the guest parlor and ushered her inside.

Even before Mr. T wheeled his chair around to face her, Virginia's tight shoulders had already relaxed. She loved these dark, silent rooms. No loud noises, no strange smells, no hustle and bustle. Walking in here was like stepping into her private chamber at the castle. Quiet, cozy, and peaceful.

"You forgot to give your coat to Swinton," her patient growled. He was wearing the bandages again.

She stepped forward to remove the strips of cloth. "I didn't forget. I never take off my coat in other people's houses."

He scowled up at her. "Why not?"

"It's easier." She deposited the bandages in a linen basket. "I never know if they'll want me to stay long enough to bother."

A muscle worked in his jaw. "Take it off when you're here."

She hesitated before removing her pelisse. Mr. T might feel that way now, but she had arrived only a few moments earlier. She would keep her coat on hand just in case.

"What do you do when you're not here?" he asked. "Pianoforte?"

She shook her head. Her sisters had been the ones who enjoyed banging at the keys at all hours of the day or night. "I've just come from the aviary."

His dark brows rose. "There's an aviary?"

She nodded. "At the castle. It's beautiful. You should see it before they change everything."

His mouth twisted, and he made a gesture toward his legs. "I'm not leaving these rooms until I am as fit as I was before I went to war."

*War.*

A battle would certainly explain the injuries.

She couldn't imagine anything noisier, riskier, further from home, more crowded, more terrifying... And he had done it anyway.

Virginia had been desperate to know what had happened but liked Mr. T too much to ask who had hurt him. It was easier to keep some things in the past where they belonged.

"I'm sorry you cannot see the aviary," she said. "It's the best part of Christmas."

His brows climbed higher. "What's so wonderful about it?"

"Everything. It started with one bird and now there are fifteen."

"Fifteen whole birds?"

Every one of them a tiny miracle. "It proves one need not look magnificent at first glance in order to end up magnificent in the end."

"Can fifteen birds ever be magnificent?" he asked.

"Even a single bird can be." She tilted her head. "Have you ever held a bird in your hands?"

"I have not. Eton and Oxford have failed me."

She made a mental note to help with that, too.

A lock of dark hair fell across the unscarred side of his face.

She tried not to notice. He was distractingly handsome. The strong jaw, she suspected he shaved himself. Well-defined muscles from riding horses into battle and rolling his chair across thick carpets. He wore no cravat and one leg of his breeches had been sliced to the knee. The state of semi-undress made him seem at once more powerful and more vulnerable.

His eyes... Virginia risked a quick look. *Brown.* Her favorite color. Brown as the feathers of a grouse or a woodcock. Tea, chocolate, chestnuts, fresh-baked crusty bread. Nothing brown had ever hurt her.

She glanced up at his eyes again. They were still watching her. The back of her neck heated.

"Did you love it or hate it?" she asked. "The war, I mean."

At first, she thought he wouldn't answer.

But then he said, "Both."

She nodded. That was how she had felt at all of her battlegrounds. She hadn't known other people felt the same.

"I want you to see the aviary," she said. "It is a very peaceful place. No one ever enters."

He shook his head. "I told you—"

"Not today," she said. "When you can walk."

"When I can walk," Mr. T reminded her, "I am leaving this village."

"After you visit the aviary," she said firmly.

Before her patient could object, she knelt at his feet and began to remove his Hessians.

Mr. T tried to roll out of her reach.

When she grabbed for the wheel, her index finger crossed over his.

He froze, neither jerking his hand free nor pushing her away.

Virginia was frozen, too. She had not meant to cover his fingers with hers. It somehow felt a thousand times more intimate than redressing a wound or tugging off a boot. Possibly because it was bare skin against bare skin.

Her winter gloves were over in her coat pocket. Gentlemen's gloves either interfered with Mr. T's ability to manipulate the wheels of his chair, or he saw no point in cleaving to such formality in the private solitude of his guest quarters.

She had never realized how soft her hands were until she had his to compare them with. Hot and large and calloused, his were the sort of hand her fingertips itched to explore. Not just the finger trapped beneath hers, but all the other fingers. Virginia longed to feel the skin on the back of his hand, to trace the muscle of his arm. She jerked her fingers from his as if scalded.

He did not move away.

She forced her hands to steady so that she could remove each boot without disturbing his injured knee.

"What are you doing?"

His voice sounded as gravelly as her heart felt. As if something had kicked loose. She was not yet certain if the missing pin was the piece that held everything together.

"Stretches," she managed to respond.

"I can't put weight on it," he reminded her.

"You don't have to." She gently lifted his foot onto her lap and began to massage the tight muscles.

"My knee is the problem." He gripped the arms of his chair. "Why are you rubbing my foot?"

"Your knee will relax if the rest of you does." She continued to massage in slow, firm patterns. "Do you like how it feels?"

Even without lifting her eyes, she could feel the heat of his gaze consuming her.

He waited until she glanced up before responding. "Yes."

Her cheeks heated. She returned her focus to her task. "This is how I like to be touched. Slow and firm. Not so hard as to hurt, and not so soft as to make the flesh crawl."

"I'll be certain to remember that," he muttered. "Probably for the rest of my life."

Virginia clamped her teeth together before she could say anything else.

She could not help but feel they shared a similarity with wild birds. His plumage, bright and colorful and magnetic. Hers, dull and gray and forgettable.

He was the most beautiful stray she had ever seen. She needed to concentrate on his well-being, not the butterflies he put in her belly.

"How did you learn to do this?" Mr. T asked.

She slowly moved her massage from his foot to his calf. "I've seen muscles atrophy from disuse. Exercise is ideal, stretching is second-best, and massage will do in a pinch." She worked her hands higher, toward the cut hem of his breeches. "Mr. T?"

"For the love of…" He let out a sigh. "Just call me Theodore."

"Let me know if I hurt you. I don't mean to." She slid her fingertips beneath the gaping cut in the hem of his breeches. "Theodore."

She was no longer massaging his muscles but mapping the terrain. His knee was swollen and tender, but not grossly misshapen. She suspected its current condition was due as much to its owner trying too hard as to lingering effects from the original injury.

"Are you done?" he asked through obviously clenched teeth.

She stilled her hands in alarm. "I said to tell me if I hurt you."

"You're not hurting me." He gestured to her hand inside the leg of his breeches. "This might be worse."

She lowered her hands back to his calf. "What is your favorite soup?"

He stared at her. "My favorite what?"

"Steaming bowls of soup are lovely on cold days." As she massaged, she lifted his foot an inch higher and then lowered it back down. "Mine is white soup with poached eggs."

"Mine is chestnut soup." He narrowed his eyes. "What does that have to do with—"

"Tea with milk or sugar?" This time as she massaged, she lifted his foot a tiny bit higher before lowering it again.

"Neither," he said. "But I'll take a pupton of apples if you have it."

Excellent choice. Who didn't love any dessert made with spices and baked apples?

"French sauces," she said. "Which is your favorite?"

"I've always been partial to—*Aargh.*" He sucked in a sharp breath. "What are you doing?"

She lowered his foot a fraction. "Right there. Do you feel that?"

"In my bones," he answered. "I thought you were trying to relax my muscles, not rip them apart."

"Relaxing was step one. Step two is to stretch. Do ten a day, ten times a day. Just this high. Enough to ache, but not hurt."

"Should I do a hundred in a row if I can stand it?"

"No," she said sharply. "If you push too hard, you'll do more damage than good. Never more than ten in an hour. Never more than ten sets a day. Do you understand the rules?"

He arched a brow. "Are you sure you've never been a military officer?"

"Never once," she said. "But you're not my first rescue."

His eyes narrowed. "How many gentlemen *have* you done this with?"

"Just you." She collected his boot and pushed to her feet. "Stop wearing these. You're giving an unnecessary shock to your knee every time you put it on or take it off."

His dark eyes flashed. "Should I take off anything else, commander?"

She rather wished he would. He could only get more attractive.

Virginia turned away before he could spy the heat on her cheeks, only to color further when she caught sight of the covered basket left abandoned just inside the door.

Poor Duke. She had forgotten all about him! She hurried over to the basket and flung open the lid.

He bared his teeth. Apparently, disturbing him had ruined his nap.

"The cat?" she heard Theodore mutter. "I was hoping for more ice cream."

Virginia reached for Duke.

He circumvented her arms and dashed instead toward the wheels of Theodore's chair. She hurried over and held out her hands.

Duke slid beneath the wheeled chair and rubbed his tail against the leather underside. When she knelt to reach for him, Duke hissed in displeasure. Rather than come to her as he had every other day since she'd rescued him, Duke curled between Theodore's feet and closed his eyes.

Virginia's confusion and hurt was quickly replaced by understanding and admiration. Duke had not rejected her. He was *conspiring* with her.

After years of watching her work, Duke had de-cided to go where he was needed, too. This was their patient. They were a team.

"Duke's right," she said as she pushed to her feet.

Theodore's brows shot up. "You speak 'meow?'"

"He speaks *my* language." Neither of them could resist a stray.

Virginia's heart pounded at what she was about to do. Duke was her oldest, most faithful compan-ion. When she had had no one, he stayed with her. He had changed her life. Gave her a reason to look forward to each day.

She forced herself to meet Theodore's eyes. Right now, he needed a friend even more than she did. And Duke had made his choice.

She took a deep breath. "I'll loan you my cat."

"Do not loan me your cat." He rolled backward. "I unconditionally reject your kind offer."

"He's loyal and diverting." She gazed down at Duke with affection. "He thinks he's a dog."

"He's a cat."

"I never told him." She would miss him like mad. "He loves to take afternoon constitutionals."

"I can't walk," Theodore reminded her.

"Duke also enjoys sleeping. And hiding."

"Now I have to hunt for him?"

"Not really. He comes when he is called."

"I doubt it," her patient scoffed.

She cracked open the door.

Duke immediately streaked from the parlor and down the corridor.

"Go ahead," Theodore said. "Call him. Impress me with Duke's dog-like grasp of proper behavior."

Virginia lowered herself to the floor and cupped her hand to her mouth. *"Duke... Duke..."*

After a short moment, he slunk around the corner, claws out, fur up, teeth bared in a hiss.

"See?" She pulled Duke into her arms and scratched behind his ears until he purred. "Model of decorum."

Theodore stared at her. "Your cat literally comes when you call, solely for the opportunity to hiss his displeasure?"

"He knows his name." She pressed a kiss between Duke's furry ears. "Makes him easy to find."

"He does not know his name. He thinks 'duke' means 'ruffle my fur and hiss.'"

Virginia felt her lips curve. "That's what you did when I first met you. Perhaps you're a duke, too."

"I am not," Theodore said quickly. "But now that I am back from war, I suppose I'm likely to spend Seasons in London."

Virginia patted her patient's shoulder without putting Duke down. "That sounds horrible."

London was a den of vipers. She had nothing but sympathy for anyone forced to survive in its midst for longer than an hour. Her pulse raced at the memory. Loud, smelly, noisy, scary, bumpy, judgmental, horrid. She would not wish such hell on anyone.

"I'll manage," Theodore said dryly. "My friends

and family are there. They look forward to seeing me." He paused. "My friends, anyway."

Interesting. Another point they shared in common.

Virginia loved her friends. She had three very good ones: Noelle, Penelope, and Gloria. They were a large part of what made Christmas feel so much like home.

Family, however... Virginia had been much better off ever since she escaped the asylum.

"Can you at least avoid the beau monde?" she asked.

"Afraid not," he said dryly.

She cuddled Duke close to keep the shivers at bay. Nothing was scarier than the *haut ton*.

Thousands of perfect, elegant people with high expectations, who believed themselves placed upon this earth to point out each other's flaws and rule over the rest.

Worst of all, the smart set preferred to do so in crowded, noisy places, filled with the stench of too many perfumes and the elbows of too many bodies and the glittering lights of too many crystal chandeliers. All that, whilst being expected to live up to an unwritten standard.

If London was Virginia's personal hell, Christmas was heaven on earth.

Here, she was not required to attend any gatherings unless she so wished. She was free to stick to quiet corners, or to stay close to a good friend. If the public dining area was too loud, the kitchen could send a tray to her room. Or she could enjoy a light repast in the park, surrounded by nature.

She didn't have to make herself perfect for Christmas. Christmas was already perfect for her.

"Is that why you want to attend the Season?" she asked. "You miss your friends?"

"And to officially ask for the hand of my intended," he admitted.

Her stomach dropped. "You have an intended?"

"No." His face twisted. "Not yet. Our fathers planned the match without our consent when we were children."

"Why consent now?"

"Father wants what is best for—" Theodore cleared his throat. "My responsibility is to secure a perfect wife. Beatrice will be one. We'll do as duty requires."

*Beatrice.*

Virginia cuddled Duke close. She had not wanted to know the intended's name.

Nor had she wished to know that Theodore considered acquiring a "perfect" wife to be a reasonable and achievable goal. He had managed to find this wonder of womanhood decades ago. An incredible length of time. Longer than any one person had ever stayed in Virginia's life.

"Do you love her?" she asked softly.

"No," he answered without hesitation. "She holds no tender feelings for me, either. It doesn't matter. Once we have sons, we'll both be free to do as we please."

Virginia was aware that members of Society did not often wed for love, and that many harbored no pretenses toward monogamy, so long as one was properly discreet about one's extramarital activities.

Her heart twisted to think that such a future was all that awaited Theodore. He was nicer than the rest. He deserved to find a wife who liked him. Someone he liked in return.

"Is that why you are in a hurry to heal?" she asked. "Because she's expecting you in London?"

"I am in a hurry to heal because half my body hurts like the devil. As for London..." He tightened his jaw for a long moment. "Are you able to keep a secret?"

"I often *am* the secret." She sat Duke on the floor. "What do you need?"

His brow furrowed, but then he pulled a folded letter from inside his jacket. "Can you hide this in your basket and post it from the castle without anyone seeing you?"

"Of course." She scooped up her empty basket and slipped the letter inside. "I'll do so at once."

Even if it was a letter to Beatrice.

Virginia retrieved her coat and hurried from the room before she could change her mind.

She set down the basket by the front door only long enough to slip her arms into her coat and fasten the buttons, then picked up the basket and made her way back up the hill.

Halfway to the castle, she could not stand the suspense any longer. She fished the letter from the basket and flipped it over to read the direction.

The neat penmanship did not say "Beatrice" anything. The letter was addressed to a Lord Ramsbury.

Virginia shoved it back into the basket in embarrassment. She should not have looked. Who Theodore chose to correspond with should not signify.

Yet she was filled with more questions than ever.

She jogged up the final steps to the castle entrance and all but ran directly into her bosom friend Penelope and her new husband, Nicholas.

Penelope's eyes lit up. "Off on a constitutional with Duke? I doubt he gets much exercise trapped inside a basket."

"Nor can a bird fly inside a golden cage," Virginia stammered. She hoped Penelope would not have more questions about where she had been. "Were you looking for me?"

Nicholas grinned. "We were doing biscuit reconnaissance. Penelope with her notebook and I with my stomach."

Virginia tried not to be hurt that they had not been looking for her after all.

"Have you heard of a Lord Ramsbury?" she blurted out.

"Is he here?" Nicholas glanced over his shoulder. "The marquess is a cold fish, but his son is a standup fellow. Honest, clever, well-respected. Good chap."

"Is he here?" she asked.

Nicholas shook his head. "Lord Ormondton is off on the continent fighting Boney."

Lord Ormondton.

Theodore was *titled*.

Virginia felt the blood drain from her face.

He wasn't being tossed into High Society like a minnow into a pool of piranhas. He *was* High Society.

Penelope gave her husband an affectionate smile. "Perhaps your friend will be back by the time we get to London."

Virginia stomach sank further. "You're going to London?"

"Nicholas is used to spending the Season in town," Penelope explained. "Now that Noelle is there, too, I thought it would be nice to pay her a visit."

Virginia nodded. She missed their good friend, too. Virginia had just hoped Noelle would return to Christmas, not that all her other friends would leave as well.

Her heart pounded. Everyone said friendship was forever, but for Virginia it had not been. Everyone said family was forever, and for Virginia it had not been. Everyone said a mother's love was forever. For Virginia, it had been the first to go.

She didn't get to have the same things as everyone else.

# CHAPTER 5

*T*heo gritted his teeth as he stretched his leg in another round of the movements Virginia had prescribed.

He had doubted their potential effectiveness and dreaded the inevitable pain, but to his surprise, his muscles gradually grew more limber and the pain slightly more tolerable.

Even if the pain had increased, Theo would have continued with the stretches for as long as they seemed to increase his strength. His jaw clenched. He would always be scarred and perhaps always limp, but he would be damned before he allowed himself to be weak.

Yet the biggest surprise of all had nothing to do with the slow but steady recuperation of his ravaged body.

Normally, whenever he needed to distance his mind from something that caused him pain, he would block out the rest of the world and recite verses of poetry. He'd all but memorized every stanza of his most cherished possession, a leather-bound book of poems by Matilda Bethem.

But he hadn't needed the familiar escape in order to withstand today's stretches. He'd forgotten about poetry altogether. All he could think about was Virginia.

She occupied his thoughts even when he did not wish to be distracted. When he shaved his jaw, tied his neckcloth, drank his tea… There she was, filling his head. The more he tried to push her from his mind, the more indelible her image became. Her face was the last thing he remembered before drifting off to sleep at night. He rather suspected she had even visited in his dreams.

Of course, any peace she had brought him shattered when her cat had awakened Theo by licking the good side of his face.

Right now, the beast was sneaking atop the dressing table to lap at the bowl of ice meant for Theo's knee.

He rolled his chair over to shoo the cat away. After wrapping the ice in a cloth, he pressed it to his knee.

Duke glared up at him balefully, no doubt plotting his revenge. When Theo least expected, the stealthy beast would spring from some darkened hiding spot and lave his rough tongue across the back of Theo's ankle or the lobe of Theo's ear or whatever other terrifying spot Duke found amusing to dampen with cat saliva.

"Don't even think about it," Theo warned. "Behave. We're stuck together."

It was true enough. Throughout his life, Theo

had prided himself on never having broken a promise. His word was very much his bond. He was careful not to give it if there was the slightest doubt of following through. Honor could not be broken.

Although he had taken care to make no promises with regard to tolerating Virginia's intolerable cat, he could not bring himself to treat the beast with any less respect than the creature expected from his mistress. Not out of any particular affection for the misanthropic Duke, but because Theo did not wish to disappoint Virginia. Even if she would never know.

The bowl that had held the ice now only contained a small quantity of cold water.

"Very well." Theo lifted the porcelain dish from the side table and scooted it across the carpet toward the cat. "Ice for me, water for the duke."

Rather than graciously accept this offering, Duke extended his claws and hissed. Eyes glinting at Theo, Duke bared his teeth for an extended moment and then fled the room as if the devil himself had given chase.

"Bloody cat really does know his name," Theo muttered. The teeth-baring hiss was an impressive trick by itself, but the extra second Duke paused to gloat before running away elevated the insult to a masterful level.

Swinton appeared in the open doorway. "Mr. T, you have a guest. Shall I show her to your private parlor or the front drawing room?"

Theo glanced up with interest. "Is it Miss Underwood?"

"Calling cards are on the dish in the main drawing room," Swinton replied noncommittally.

Theo sent him a flat look. "Can't you just tell me?"

"Would you like me to fetch the card for you?"

"You are the butler," Theo reminded him. "Your job is to present me with guests' calling cards, or at the very least inform me of their names."

"My job is to do so for the Duke of Azureford." Swinton reached into an inner pocket and displayed the edge of his master's letter. "You, sir, don't even have a proper name."

Theo hiccupped at the reminder. Here, he wasn't Lord Ormondton. He was Mr. T.

Outranked by a butler.

"Why doesn't Azureford sack you?" he muttered.

Swinton raised his brows. "A wise master never sacks a man who recalls seeing him in nappies."

Theo snorted. He now suspected unmasking himself as a peer of the realm wouldn't give him the least advantage with Swinton.

"Do not let anyone in until I see their card," Theo said firmly.

He wheeled himself out of his shadowed chambers and down the corridor to the main drawing room. The silver platter meant to collect calling cards was in its promised spot upon the mantel. He rolled over to pull the dish into his lap.

All four of the cards were identical, which meant Virginia had presented one on every visit, despite the staff clearly knowing her well.

That was not the strange part.

Theo's brow furrowed as he picked up the topmost card. The thick, white rectangle was blank, save for the black silhouette of a single bird.

He flipped it over. Nothing on the other side. No names, no words of any kind. Just the featureless outline of a small bird. Frowning, he flipped over all the cards. Four black birds; nothing else.

Theo kept the cards and placed the dish back upon the mantel. "Please inform Miss Underwood—"

Soft footsteps sounded as Virginia swept into the room, a wicker basket dangling from one hand.

Apparently, Swinton had taken *Don't show anyone in until I see their card* literally. Theo had seen the card. Now the guest was in.

Theo craned his neck toward the closest footman. "Please close the curtains. I do not want passers-by spying inside."

The footman set about the task immediately.

Theo turned to Virginia. "Please take a seat wherever you like."

She chose a chair in front of one of Azureford's decorative folding screens.

Theo wheeled himself directly opposite to face her. "Why do your calling cards contain an image of a bird and absolutely no information about you?"

She lifted a dainty shoulder. "Everyone who knows me already knows how to find me."

"What about the people who don't know you?" he pointed out.

Her eyes widened. "Why would I want strangers to find me?"

Well. No arguing with that. Theo glanced down at the four cards in his hands.

"What are they? Crows? Ravens? Blackbirds?"

"Colly birds," Virginia's gaze slid away from him. "A few people say 'calling birds,' but the correct term is 'colly' like coal, due to their black feathers. They're very striking against the snow."

"Of course," Theo murmured. Only Virginia would have a calling bird for a calling card.

As always, the outside air had brought a becoming flush to her cheeks and lips. She was once again wearing the forest green pelisse she'd been sporting the first time he saw her.

"Swinton." Theo lifted his eyes to the butler. "Could you please guard Miss Underwood's outerwear?"

Her gaze met his briefly. A small smile flicked at the edges of her lips. As if she had not been certain of her welcome but was pleased it had been extended.

He would not tell her that, since waking, he had spent every moment waiting for her to call.

"How are your wounds?"

"Improving," he said with relief. "Progress is slow but unquestionable. How was your constitutional?"

"One does not need to see the sun shining overhead to feel warmed by its light." She glanced about the parlor. "How is Duke?"

"Also a ray of sunshine," Theo said dryly.

"Good." She sat back. "It is important to have moments of sunshine."

*She* was the ray of sun, not her irascible cat. "Did you post my letter?"

Virginia nodded. "As soon as I reached the castle."

He waited.

She said nothing else. Asked no questions; treated him no differently. She did not seem to have deduced a connection between the name on the letter and the anonymous gentleman seated across from her.

Theo's tight shoulders relaxed. Excellent.

His parents would have proof he was still alive, but no details on where he had chosen to convalesce. He could heal in peace. As for everyone else, it was better for them to assume Theo still off at war until he was healthy enough to take his place among the beau monde again.

At which point, he would also deal with Lady Beatrice. But until then...

"What's in the basket?" he asked.

Her face lit up. "A wonderful surprise."

Theo wasn't certain he could handle any more of life's surprises.

Virginia's eyes sparkled. "When you said you could not visit the aviary, I felt so sorry for you—"

"Do not feel sorry for me," he said firmly.

"—so I brought the aviary to *you.*"

Theo blinked. "You what?"

She opened the lid to the basket.

With a flutter of feathers, a large bird burst free and began flapping about the parlor.

"What," Theo asked politely, "is that supposed to be?"

"A partridge," Virginia replied. "Note the short tail and brown plumage."

"What is a partridge doing in my parlor?" he clarified.

"The Duke of Azureford's parlor," came Swinton's inflectionless voice behind him.

At this pronouncement, the cat skidded into the drawing room, hissed at everyone present, and dashed out.

Virginia beamed at Theo in satisfaction. "Now you have a reason for an afternoon constitutional."

"I do?" he asked with dread.

"Azureford has an outbuilding just behind the cottage. It would make a splendid temporary home for a partridge. Swinton has agreed to store Dancer there for the duration of your visit."

Theo cast the butler a flat look over his shoulder. "Swinton is all that is kind and thoughtful."

"All you have to do is go outside and feed him," she continued.

He jerked his head back to Virginia. "You expect me to *what?*"

She pulled a fat pouch from the basket and set it atop the tea table. "A small handful every afternoon should do. Let me know when you run out of seeds, and I'll bring more."

"You expect me to wheel myself outside, in the snow, to an outbuilding, which will now contain a bird I did not ask for, in order to feed it seeds from the palm of my hand?" Theo asked in disbelief.

She shook her head. "Just toss them on the ground. Dancer gets excited when he eats, and his little pecks can hurt."

"I won't do it," Theo said. There was too much risk of someone spotting him in his current condition. Nor did he wish to appear weak in front of the entire staff. "I'll send a footman."

"I've already asked them not to help you," she said. "It's your afternoon constitutional."

"*You* do not command the staff. Until Azureford returns, I am the one who—"

"Not according to this." Virginia pulled a suspiciously familiar folded letter from inside the basket.

Theo glared over his shoulder at Swinton. "You showed her Azureford's instructions?"

The butler gazed back at him impassively.

Virginia unfolded the letter. "I read very well. You are not to be molly-coddled. Azureford says so, and I concur."

Theo held out his hand. "Give me the letter."

Swinton swept between them and plucked the paper from Virginia's hand before she could relinquish it to Theo. "You shall not toss my master's correspondence into the fire."

Theo narrowed his eyes. "That's where it belongs."

Swinton affected a placid smile. "I am certain a grateful guest would never imply that his wishes outranked those of my master, the duke."

At once, Virginia's cat streaked into the room, hissed at them all, paused for effect, and ran off.

"Never say 'duke,'" Theo said wearily.

Swinton tucked the letter safely inside his jacket and quit the room.

"Can you send someone to fetch the bird?" Theo called after him. "He belongs in an out-building."

"Partridge," Virginia corrected. "His name is Dancer."

Dancer perched atop one of Azureford's decorative folding screens. Theo hoped the delicate design wasn't about to get even more decorative.

Virginia rose from her chair, stepping forward until the soft folds of her gown rustled between Theo's legs.

"I told you," she said softly. "No more hiding your wounds. They need to breathe."

Theo wasn't hiding his wounds. He was hiding himself. Protecting others from being frightened by a beast.

She unwrapped the thin strips of cloth from his face. "Don't do it again. Have you more bandages somewhere?"

He would not lie to her, so he said nothing.

Virginia strode from the drawing room and returned bearing the spare rolls of cloth strips that had been on the dressing table in Theo's guest chamber.

He wondered if she'd sent a footman or if she walked in herself. Perhaps when he entered, the room would now smell like Virginia.

She tossed the bandages into her basket and closed the lid.

He sighed. "Are you ever going to bring ice cream again?"

"When you earn it," she replied. "Does your face feel better without all that cloth covering it?"

His face did not feel better. His misshapen countenance felt naked. Exposed. Ghastly.

If Virginia found him as such, she made no sign. She neither recoiled from his wounds nor twisted her face in disgust. Instead, she cupped her hand to his good cheek.

"Scars aren't evidence of failure," she said softly. "They are proof of survival."

Any brusque response he might have given tangled in his chest at her gentleness. He lifted his hand to cover hers. She had not just seen through the bandages, but understood his fears, his doubts, his guilt. And washed them all away with a touch and an insightful word.

How did she know so much? His blood pulsed faster. Had someone hurt her?

"Do you have a scar?" He meant the question to be as warm and protective as her hand on his face, but the words clawed from his throat in a growl.

Without answering the question, she slipped her fingers from beneath his and sank to her knees. "I am pleased you are no longer wearing those useless Hessians."

"Yes, well." He gestured at their replacement. "Dancing slippers are just as unnecessary."

She slipped them off and began to massage his muscles. "You feel even better this time."

Theo tightened his jaw. *She* felt better every time she touched him. It was as if his flesh not only remembered her hands but yearned for them. He melted into each stroke. He would do anything she asked as long as she kept touching him.

"Tell me about the castle," he said gruffly. "Do you like living here?"

"I love it," she answered.

At first, he thought that was all Virginia would say on the matter. But then she took a deep breath and continued.

"It has everything I love in one place. My friends, my animals, my quiet chambers. There are seventy-two steps to my floor, with a sconce every twelve-step. The candles are lit, but subdued. Bright enough to light the way yet not garish enough to dazzle the eyes. The landing at the south tower has the best view of the stars. In the kitchen at sunrise, the day's bread is just leaving the oven. It smells divine."

He considered her words. "You dislike bright light?"

"Don't you?" she asked. "Your rooms are kept at the perfect ambience. The fire in this parlor is cozy, not roaring. Instead of lighting the chandelier overhead, there are a few candelabra throughout the parlor. I can gaze at you without being distracted by flames."

Theo swallowed. From the moment she entered the room, he had stopped being conscious of any other sources of beauty. He could only gaze at her.

"You notice details other people might not," he said in admiration. "Seventy-two steps. Sconces every twelve. The right moment to catch fresh bread exiting the oven."

She kept massaging his leg. "Doesn't everyone pay attention to the things they like?"

"Maybe you like more things than everyone else." He could not tear his eyes from her. "Maybe you appreciate life more."

"I like liking things," she said with a shrug. "I like the tiny pink pads of my cat's paws. I like wind in my face on my afternoon constitutionals. I like the squeak of your front door when Swinton lets me in."

"The squeaking of *Azureford's* front door," Theo said firmly. "Don't fill my head with notions that I am master of anything."

"You are master of yourself. I'll prove it." She leapt to her feet.

His body immediately mourned the loss of her hands.

She dragged the folding screen without a partridge and placed it halfway between the parlor door and Theo's wheeled chair.

"Roll forward until you can touch the screen with your toes."

He gave up on stoicism and rolled himself to the center of the folding screen until his toes bumped into the panel.

"Good," she said. "Back up an inch."

He did so.

"Now touch it with your toes."

Easy enough.

"Good," she said again. "Back up another inch."

Theo began to suspect this game was not going to end well for him. He did as requested inch by inch until the pain of stretching higher won out over the rush of victory from pushing through.

"Stop," she scolded him. "I told you. Do as much as you can, and not the slightest bit more. We're stretching your muscles, not reinjuring them. Now don't move."

She pulled a measuring rule from her wicker basket.

He raised his brows. "You carry a measuring device everywhere you go?"

Ignoring him, she knelt between his chair and the screen. "Remember this number. Today you achieved—"

A knock sounded on the front door on the other side of the corridor.

Seconds later, the cottage filled with the merry sound of a dozen or more carolers singing *Here We Come a-Wassailing* in harmony.

The measuring rule fell from Virginia's hand. She shrank back, her derrière landing on the carpet in surprise.

No. Not surprise. Something closer to panic. Theo frowned. Her face had blanched, her muscles trembled, her eyes were shut tight.

"Send them away!" he roared.

For once, Swinton did not argue.

The caroling stopped.

Virginia did not move.

Theo wished he could pull her into his lap. He cupped her pale face in his hands instead.

"They're gone," he said softly.

She remained impossibly still for another long moment. At last, she let out a long breath and rested her cheek against the palm of his hand. "I'm sorry."

Her voice was hesitant and shaky. As if his potential reaction terrified her more than the carolers.

"Do not apologize." He stroked her cheek with the pad of his thumb. "They startled you. It's April, not December."

She shook her head. "It's Christmas. Year-round."

He frowned. "I thought you loved it here."

"I do. There are fewer loud noises here than anywhere else I've ever been." She opened her eyes, but her gaze did not meet his. "Loud noises are hard. Sudden changes are hard. Crowds are very hard. It's easier if I know it's coming. And if I have a friend with me." Her shoulders slumped. "They have been busy lately, so I've been trying to make do on my own. Some days are easier than others."

"I'm your friend," he said gruffly. "I am never too busy for you."

She shook her head. "You said you weren't my friend. You wanted me to go away."

"I'm an imbecile," he said. "I regretted it the moment I said it."

"You can't be with me always," she said after a moment. "No one will. I have to learn not to startle on my own."

She was right. He wished she wasn't.

He wished he could promise to be the person she could count on when life startled or scared her.

As friends, of course.

He lowered his hand from her face.

She lifted her gaze. "Are you disappointed in me?"

"Do I look disappointed to you?" he asked in surprise. She was one of the most compassionate, resilient, resourceful women he had ever met. The sort who would bring a man his own aviary, so he could have a small piece of the joy it brought her.

"I don't know." Her voice was small. "It's hard to know what others are thinking. That's why I asked. I don't want to disappoint you."

"You have never disappointed me," he said, his voice firm. "When I told you to go away that first day, it was because I wanted to protect you from *me*."

She bit her lip as if considering that possibility.

Theo tried to imagine how difficult it would be to interact with the world if he were never certain what would happen next or whether he was making someone sad or angry or disappointed.

It would be exhausting, to say the least. Possibly even terrifying at times.

He did not want to be one of the things that scared her.

"Listen to me." He touched her hand. "I take honor very seriously. I give you my word never to become upset with you over any perceived awkwardness or miscommunication."

Her gaze flicked up to his too quickly for him to determine what she was thinking.

"You explained your position beautifully," he continued. "From this moment on, I take full responsibility for my part of communicating effectively. If you need something, just tell me." He touched his knuckle beneath her chin. "You're safe."

She lifted her face up toward his, her green eyes luminous and irresistible. She licked her lips.

He was not strong enough to haul her up from her knees and into his lap—admittedly, a terrible idea—but if they both leaned forward a few inches, their mouths would be close enough to touch.

An equally terrible idea, he reminded himself firmly.

And yet he was locked in place by the war raging inside him. The desire to embrace her, to comfort her, to forget everything else with a kiss. He had never wanted anything so badly.

He had to force himself not to reach for her. The sensation was both intoxicating and alarming. Theo had never experienced desire toward Lady Beatrice. He had always intended to beget the requisite heir and spare and then leave her alone. Passion was not why they would wed. He had convinced himself it was not something he would notice lacking from his marriage.

But with Virginia... Good God. He was drawn to everything. Wanted more. He could barely look at her without his heart racing at the temptation to cover her mouth with his.

Friends, he reminded himself. He could not allow an infatuation. Or anything more.

He could not let Virginia sense his attraction.

Future marquesses did what they must, not what they wished.

She sprang to her feet. "I'm all right. I'll return tomorrow. Don't worry, we'll have you back to your betrothed in no time."

"She is not my betrothed," his traitorous mouth blurted. "I've made no such promise."

Virginia scooped up her basket. "You will as soon as you're on your feet."

She had him there.

"Yes," he admitted. "She will be, once I'm on my feet. What about you? Have you an intended?"

Her eyes rounded as though he had asked whether she fancied a nice dive into a pool filled with spiders. "I'll never marry."

He couldn't imagine that. "You haven't found someone who interests you? Or—"

"I don't want to," she said quickly. "And don't worry. I've no interest in marrying you."

She disappeared around the folding screen. Moments later, the sound of the front door indicated her departure.

*I've no interest in marrying you.*

He glanced down at his useless leg, touched his hand to the uneven contours of his face. Of course she wouldn't be interested.

A warm homecoming might not await him in London, either.

# CHAPTER 6

*I*n the week since the carolers had forced Virginia to bare a few of her secrets, she had taken great care to treat Theodore with utmost professionalism and not expose any more of her flaws.

A difficult task, at times.

She ran her fingers along the mahogany shelves of the castle library. This was where she always came when she didn't know where else to go. Quiet, cozy, and out of the way, the library was filled with an abundance of books and no other distractions.

Shelves like these had taught her almost everything she knew. Her favorites were the tomes on nature. If a book pertained to flora or fauna, Virginia had read it countless times. Should the situation come up, she would know exactly what to do if she came across a wild hog, or wished to start an orchid garden, or wondered if a mushroom would be delicious or deadly.

Unfortunately, no such instructional manuals

existed on the subject of pleasing one's family. Not making a fool of oneself in public situations. Attracting suitors or rebuffing rakes. How to be the only unmarried woman in one's circle of friends. What to do when one found oneself left behind. How to comport oneself with one's patient, when all one secretly wished to do was press her lips to his in a decidedly unprofessional kiss.

She would not, of course. Not unless she was certain that he wanted to kiss her, too.

She slumped her shoulders against the closest shelf. That was the problem, was it not? All she ever had were doubts. What did he think? What did he feel? What did he want? She clenched her fingers. How was anybody supposed to tell?

Her eyes focused on a row of nature journals before her. Theodore had asked her about birds. Was he interested in ornithology? She slid the small volume from its spot on the shelf and slipped it into her reticule. Enough dillydallying. It was time to visit her patient.

But as she navigated the stands of books, another spine caught her attention. *Debrett's Peerage & Baronetage.* A compendium containing the names of the nobility and everyone who mattered. She ignored it, as she did every other time its spine screamed at her from the shelves. She did not need to know anything it contained. She would not be returning to London or hobnobbing with titled folk. When she bid *adieu* to Theodore, her life would return to normal.

As normal as it ever was.

She stopped by her private chamber for her

pelisse and basket before heading down the spiral staircase toward the castle exit.

Before she reached the door, the castle solicitor stepped into her path.

"Miss Underwood," he said. "You more than anyone will be delighted to hear my news."

Last time he had news, Virginia had been anything but delighted. The solicitor seemed as bad as she was at guessing others' thoughts.

"What is it?" she forced herself to ask.

He beamed at her. "I am in possession of Mr. Marlowe's complete plans for the aviary. All the moving pieces are finally underway. Not only will all that wasted space be fully stocked within a month, we are hiring an expert."

"An expert?"

"A veterinarian," he explained. "A man with years of experience, specializing in the care of birds. I shan't be surprised if the aviary becomes the most popular attraction for miles."

Virginia's flesh turned cold. It wasn't just that the castle was replacing her with someone better. They planned to turn her beloved sanctuary into a tourist spot filled with noise and people.

And it would happen within the month.

"Thank you for warning me," she managed.

The solicitor frowned. "There will be hundreds of new birds. Aren't you—"

But Virginia was already pushing away from him, away from the suddenly oppressive confines of the expansive receiving room with its high arched walls.

The castle was changing. Soon there would be no room for her.

As she stepped out into the wintry afternoon, she sucked in a breath of cold, bracing air. The bright sun overhead was blanketed by soft clouds, diffusing the light. It was not warm enough for snow to melt nor cold enough for new flakes to fall. No breeze rustled through the white-dusted trees. The day was perfectly still and quiet, as if nothing was happening at all.

She recognized a calm before a storm. If she was no longer needed in the aviary, if the castle was about to be overrun with even bigger crowds, what did she intend to do?

With her heavy basket in her arms, she set a brisk pace down the lane and tried to devise a viable plan.

At least she wasn't indigent. When Mr. Marlowe had taken her in as his ward, he had provided her with monthly pin money. When he died, his will and testament had set aside a dowry in her name.

Which meant, quite possibly, Virginia was one of the few young ladies in all of England to possess not one, but two dowries.

She was not certain if the original dowry her parents had provided still existed, but it did not matter. She had no intention to marry. Doing so would give her husband the same power her parents had wielded—the ability to commit her to an asylum against her will for the rest of her life. Spinsterhood was by far the better path.

In the six years that she'd been receiving her monthly allowance, Virginia had made very few purchases. It wasn't necessary. Lodgings were provided. Meals were provided. The castle library held a plethora of books and more arrived every year.

Her unused pin money had snowballed into a significant sum.

Now could be the time to spend it. She strode faster. This was the push she needed. Her chance to open the animal sanatorium she'd dreamed of owning.

She would cease to be the specter in the castle. She'd be as demonstrably useful in her domain as the exalted bird expert would be to the castle aviary. She wouldn't just *have* something important. She would *be* important.

That was, if Virginia could manage the non-animal aspects of operating a sanatorium. There would be so many people to talk to. So many ways it could go wrong.

She would need an appropriate venue. To negotiate terms. Sign a contract. Commission furnishings. She would either need to seek out animals in need on her own time or solicit business from other residents. From *strangers*.

Oh, who was she bamming? She would never leave the castle. The fragrant basket in her arms seemed heavier than ever.

Swinton answered her knock.

"Don't announce me yet," she whispered. "This is for my patient, although he needn't know it is from me."

Swinton ushered her into the entryway and closed the door. "What have you brought?"

"Ingredients." She lifted the lid to allow him a peek. "Mr. T adores chestnut soup and pupton of apples. He should have it as a reward for dogged perseverance."

"You could have provided us with a menu and saved yourself time and money," Swinton chided her as he accepted the basket.

She could have, yes, but Virginia had enjoyed shopping for Theodore's favorite foods. Spending her pin money on ingredients was a distant second to hand-preparing a home-cooked meal, but for a moment it allowed her to believe she could offer something special.

Swinton bowed. "I'll take this to the kitchen."

Virginia crossed to the corridor and paused. Swinton had not mentioned where to find her patient. Theodore could be in the front parlor, in his private drawing room, anywhere at all.

Self-consciously, she tiptoed into the primary drawing room.

She hoped Swinton would warn her if the Duke of Azureford were also at home, but all the same, it was best not to go barging about like a herd of elephants.

After having determined that Theodore was not at the front of the cottage, she headed toward the rear.

Near the guest quarters, voices spilled from an open door. She froze just out of view. Did Theodore have company? Should she leave, rather than intrude?

"I would not have dreamed it, sir," came a male voice she did not recognize. "I'd come to think of you and that chair as nigh inseparable."

"That's because you've feathers for brains," came the warm, familiar growl that heated Virginia to her toes. "Miss Underwood never doubted. You could learn a thing or two from someone as wise as her."

Virginia's breath caught. He thought her wise?

"Am I to join you on her visits?" the young male voice asked.

"You are not," came Theodore's laconic reply. "Mind yourself. And watch out for the—"

"Is that devil-cat hiding right behind me?" The words tumbled forth in a rush. "Is Duke going to—"

A loud hiss rent the air.

Virginia grinned.

"I'm sorry, sir," the lad babbled. "You said never to say 'duke' and now I've gone and said 'duke' and—"

Another hiss from her clever cat.

Virginia's smile wobbled. Perhaps she was the only one who understood Duke's charms. Perhaps Theodore would rather—

"Don't apologize," came his voice. "If that abhorrent creature hadn't infiltrated the cottage, I wouldn't have Miss Underwood."

Her heart melted. She owed Duke a lifetime of treats for that trick.

"But, sir, you said you didn't wish to talk to anyone at all."

"I don't want to talk to anyone but her," came

the terse reply. "Don't you have somewhere else to be?"

Eek! Virginia backed away double-time. She made a point of letting her feet fall in heavy steps as she neared the open door once more.

"She's here!" came the lad's excited whisper.

"I have ears," Theodore replied.

Virginia stepped into the doorway as if she'd overheard nothing. "Good afternoon! I've—"

Her jaw fell open. Theodore was on his crutches!

She rushed into the room, her hands clasped together in delight. "You're doing it!"

"Of course I'm doing it," he growled. "It was your idea and is therefore your fault."

"This is marvelous," she told him. "*You* are marvelous."

"*You're* marvelous," he countered, and immediately pulled a face. "Lad, are you still here?"

The boy dashed from the room.

"My valet," Theodore said. "I can't tell if he wants to be my protégé or my mother."

She came closer. "How long have you been using the crutches?"

"About an hour." He gave a crooked smile. "There's a partridge expecting me in the outbuilding. I thought I'd take my afternoon constitutional on foot today."

"Take it slow," she warned him. "It might be best if your first steps on crutches don't involve uneven terrain and patches of ice."

His jaw tightened. "I don't want to take it slow. I want to be *better*."

"Every day I've visited, you've been better than the last," she pointed out. "You'll be yourself again in no time."

It was bittersweet. Theodore improved every single day. And the moment he was well enough to leave her... He *would*.

"I'm proud of you," she said, despite the lump in her throat. "This isn't just one of the steps in the process to recovery. It's one of the last big obstacles."

He brightened. "Did you bring ice cream to celebrate?"

"I didn't know I'd find you on your feet." She hesitated, then opened her reticule. "I brought you this instead."

He accepted the slim volume from her. "A book?"

Her heart sank. "Is it a stupid gift?"

"I love books." Theodore flipped the volume over to inspect it. "And I have never read... *The Naturalist's Miscellany or Coloured Figures of Natural Objects; Drawn and Described Immediately From Nature.*"

"It's from the castle library," she admitted. "You'll have to return it before you go."

He clutched it to his chest. "When the time comes, I shall summon the personal fortitude required to part with it."

She nodded. "Although sketched illustrations are a feeble representation of the wonders of life, sometimes pen and ink are more than enough to transport us from our own life into another."

He tilted his head. "Are you always so poetic?"

"Poetic?" she stammered in confusion.

*Odd* was how most people described her. Eccentric. Random. Awkward. Peculiar.

"I like how you see the world," he said. "I want to think in clever metaphors, but the talent eludes me. You have a gift."

Talent.

He thought her *gifted*.

Virginia swayed, so foreign were the compliments he was firing her way. No one had ever taken her strangeness as an advantage before, least of all Virginia.

"I…" The idea that anyone could consider any of her traits to be an enviable talent had completely robbed the breath from her lungs.

Theodore wasn't embarrassed by her. He didn't want her to change the way her mind worked. He thought she was just… Virginia. And liked her that way.

"Sit," she commanded.

Not because he was unsteady on his feet, but because *her* legs were trembling.

"I obey no one's orders but my own," he said as he eased into his wheeled chair and handed her the crutches. "I happen to be done with those anyway."

"Do not overdo it," she reminded him as she leaned the crutches against the wall. "You'll do more harm than good and be back in that chair for even longer."

"I cannot wait to be done with this chair," he muttered.

Virginia swallowed. She didn't just hope to see

him healed; she wanted to be the one who helped him. To be useful, special. To have made a difference in someone's life.

But when she managed all that—*if* she managed all that—she would hate to see him go.

"How is your knee?" She knelt at his feet and ran her hands over the muscles of his injured leg.

He scowled down at her. "How does it feel?"

Good. Warm. Strong. The muscles of his leg were more familiar than her own. She could close her eyes at night and imagine every inch beneath her palms. To do so made her wish she knew the rest of him as intimately. For her fingers to explore not just the contours of his leg, but the breadth of his shoulders, the muscles of his chest, the strength in his arms.

"Are you comfortable?" he asked quietly.

Ever since the carolers had come to call, her patient's habitual high-handed arrogance had become peppered with soft inquiries into how she felt, what she needed. Because she doubted he noticed he was doing so, each offhand question melted her heart.

Until Theodore, no one had ever asked how she would prefer the lighting or the temperature or the noise or anything at all. Everyone else either presumed they knew best or assumed her wishes exactly matched theirs.

Theodore didn't just treat her like a person. He went beyond his normal comfort and behavior in order to ensure she would not have to. It was the headiest sensation Virginia had ever experienced.

What did she want? *Him*, blast it all.

She let her hands fall.

His head jerked up. "You aren't going to massage me?"

"The swelling is gone." She bit her lip. "You don't need me to massage your knee."

He muttered something that sounded suspiciously like, "I'd want you to massage me even if I were healthy."

She started to push to her feet.

He held out a hand to help her.

She didn't need help. She took his hand anyway.

After she rose to her feet, she shook the wrinkles from her skirts. "Shall we feed Dancer?"

He narrowed his eyes. "I thought you said I must sojourn to my one-bird aviary alone."

She laughed. "I don't count."

"You count very much." He wheeled not toward the front door, but toward the servants' exit at the rear, where planks of wood had been placed just outside the door.

With a practiced movement, he launched his chair up and over the first hump and sailed down the ramp toward the outbuilding.

She smiled to herself. Theodore might not see it, but he was as capable now as he ever was. "Do you regret going to war?"

"I wish I hadn't been injured, if that's what you mean." He turned his chair around to wheel into the outbuilding backward in order to hold the door for her. "I'm not sorry I went. Helping people in need is always the right decision."

Her chest tightened. "I agree."

"If only everyone did," he muttered.

She stepped inside the outbuilding and shut the door before Dancer could escape. "Did someone say that helping people was not the right choice?"

"Everyone I know," he said flatly. "Although not in those words. Only my father put it quite so baldly. My sole responsibility is to stay alive to ensure the family home doesn't go to some country cousin."

"You haven't any brothers?" she asked.

"No siblings at all." He pulled the bag of feed to his lap and began tossing seeds near the partridge. "How about you? Are you an only child?"

She shook her head.

His eyebrows shot up. "You're not? Where's your family? Why am I just hearing about this?"

"They're not here," she said vaguely. "And you're the first one to ask."

She wished he hadn't. She was not fond of Vera, Viveca, and Valeria. And she knew good and well they were not fond of her. It was not a story she planned to share.

"You were brave to go against your parents' wishes," Virginia said instead.

"My first rebellion against Father and Society." He gestured at the chair. "Look how it turned out."

"You're alive," she said simply. "It turned out quite favorably indeed."

"It could be worse," he admitted.

She tilted her head. "You do not seem the sort who allows life to just happen."

The corner of his mouth twisted into a smile.

"I am the sort to charge in," he agreed. "The Army suited me in that regard. A cause to fight for, troops to lead. It may sound silly, but it was quite vindicating to be powerful and needed."

"Not silly at all," she whispered.

He tossed the bag of seed back to the ground and watched as Dancer clucked through her bounty in delight.

"Do you miss the war?" she asked.

"Never give up and never give in," he answered. "This injury robbed me of the choice. I did not give up and I did not give in, but I was carried from the battlefield anyway."

"With broken bones and bullet wounds," she reminded him.

"I had so much more to give." He turned to look at her. "As a respected officer, not as my father's shadow."

Virginia's heart twisted. Her case was different, but she understood the sentiment all too well. She had longed her entire life to be accepted for who she was, not rejected for who she was not.

She would run away to the war, too, if it could give her a chance to belong.

Theodore turned toward the exit of the outbuilding and pulled open the door.

When he made no move to precede her into the afternoon sun, Virginia thanked him and slipped outside.

Together, they headed back to the planks at the rear of the cottage. As she reached out to open the servants' door, his fingers brushed her free hand.

"Step to the side," he murmured. "Or he'll get you."

She pulled the handle. "*Who* will—"

Duke streaked through the crack in the door and barreled right at them.

Thanks to Theodore's suggestion, Virginia was not in his path. Duke continued past her, took two laps about Theodore's wheeled chair, and disappeared back inside.

"Ignore him," Theodore said with a sigh. "He does that."

It was all Virginia could do to keep a grin from overtaking her face.

Whether her patient realized it or not, Duke had adopted Theodore. They had a routine now. A secret handshake. A private jest only the two of them shared.

"I'm glad you get on with Duke," she said as Theodore wheeled himself inside.

"Does anyone get on with that ill-tempered beast?" he said. "I've no idea why you keep him around."

"Because he keeps coming back," she answered.

Theodore rolled to his crutches and pulled himself to his feet. "Is that why you think I keep you around?"

She pushed the chair out of his way. Their toes were nearly touching. He was now almost close enough to kiss.

"Why do you?" she asked softly.

It was a dangerous question.

He was so much larger outside of his chair. The crutches did not make him look weak, but invincible. Bullets could not stop him. Horse hooves could not stop him. Twelve scant inches of space afforded her no protection at all.

She was not trying to defend her mouth from plunder, but her heart from growing attached. All wild creatures must return where they belonged.

He reached for her and cupped her cheek with one hand.

His fingers were not the unblemished softness of an idle lord. The calluses from riding and weaponry had faded, but his touch was still rough and uneven.

Virginia loved it. She could feel his presence. Feel that it was *him*.

He dragged the pad of his thumb across her lower lip. "I want…"

A clatter rent the air as a wooden crutch banged to the ground.

He jerked upright with comical alacrity, hopping on his good foot for balance.

She swept the fallen crutch from the floor and back into his arms without meeting his eyes. Temptation had almost got the best of them. It was better not to know what might have happened if his lips had touched hers.

She would lie awake tonight wondering all the same.

"I apologize," he said. "I—"

She stepped back. "I should be helping you walk, not standing in your way. You've a grand entrance with the *ton* to look forward to."

"Grander than I'd like." He pulled a face. "I'm to

waltz with Lady Beatrice until tongues wag, then announce our betrothal."

Her stomach curdled with nausea. He needed back on his feet not just to walk again, but to dance with his future bride.

It sounded lovely. No one had ever stood up with Virginia. She tried not to be jealous of Lady Beatrice for having it. For having *him*.

"How romantic," she whispered.

"Tactical strategy," he corrected. "Lady Beatrice intends to use our betrothal as both armor and artillery."

Virginia swallowed. "And you?"

"I intend to do the same," he said. "We both know what we're getting. Improved positioning in Society is more than worth the price of a waltz." He rolled his eyes. "Ask my father."

Virginia did not need to. The imperative to improve one's perceived status at all costs had been drilled into her from the moment she could speak. It was why her parents had abandoned her to a madhouse. She was worse than useless. She was a barnacle. A mistake in need of correction.

It was not just her inability to make friends or attract suitors. Virginia had stood in her sisters' way. She tarnished their reputations with her mere existence.

Just as she would tarnish Theodore's if they were ever spotted together outside of these walls.

~

After quitting Theodore's temporary residence,

Virginia did not head straight back to the castle. No one awaited her there.

Duke was with Theodore. Mr. Marlowe was dead. Her friend Noelle had married and gone. No other permanent residents remained. Yet Virginia did not feel like being alone.

She headed instead to her friend Gloria's cottage and rapped the knocker. Gloria had fallen in love and the banns were underway, but the ceremony had not yet happened. She would still be home.

Virginia's shoulders relaxed. Unlike the others, Gloria would *always* be home. She rarely left her house, and never traveled farther than the castle. Gloria was as integral to their village as the rolling hills or the snow-frosted evergreens.

A maid answered Virginia's knock and immediately ushered her into the drawing room. Gloria was reclining on the sofa with a book. When she glimpsed Virginia, a wide smile lit Gloria's face.

"What a lovely surprise!" She pushed the book aside and sat up straight. "Shall we have tea?"

Virginia eased into the wingback chair closest to her friend. "Where's Christopher?"

Gloria's gaze filled with warmth. "I sent him to the jeweler to have new bearings designed for the orrery. He'll return within the hour, if you'd like to see him."

Virginia did not. She was glad to have a moment alone with a good friend. "Do you still read all the Society papers?"

"Dear heavens, what misdeeds are you accusing me of?" Gloria's eyes widened. "Of *course* I read the Society papers."

"What do they say about..." Virginia hesitated. She did not want to betray Theodore's secret. "... the war?"

"That it's ongoing, of course. That the French are a mix of angels and demons, Boney being the worst of the lot." Gloria shook her head. "I feel so sorry for the le Duc family, being caught in the middle."

Virginia agreed, but this was not the direction she had intended to take the conversation. She clenched her teeth. This would be so much easier if she could just *ask* what she wanted to know. How did anyone manage anything by relying on subtleties alone?

"I meant..." She cleared her throat. "...is there any mention of 'war heroes?'"

"Any mention?" Gloria fanned herself. "At least half the columns and two thirds of the caricatures are devoted to illustrating military officers and their conquests. Wellington, of course. And Ormondton. Oh, and Brigadier—"

"Ormondton?" Virginia asked.

"Lord Ormondton," Gloria clarified. "A viscount and a major. Until he left for war, Ormondton was famous for being a quick study in almost any topic, and infamous for a cutting glance apparently powerful enough to level an entire ballroom in the blink of an eye." She giggled. "How I wish I could see that!"

"But you won't?" Virginia asked.

"Not unless the war comes here," Gloria

agreed. "Ormondton is in France, wielding weapons far more dangerous than 'cutting glances.' When he returns to London, he'll have his pick of brides, and the Society papers will have to find some other strong, handsome, victorious officer to wax poetic about."

Virginia's chest tightened at the mention of brides. Theodore had chosen. Lady Beatrice was the lucky lady. And as his nurse, Virginia would do whatever it took to hurry her patient back into his intended's arms.

Even if it killed her.

## CHAPTER 7

*S*ix months ago, if one of his soldiers had asked Theo what he imagined himself doing upon his return to England, his response would *not* have been, "Loitering on crutches in the Duke of Azureford's corridor in anticipation of my self-appointed nurse, out for her afternoon constitutional."

And yet here he was.

Being able to use crutches instead of the wheeled chair was nothing short of a triumph, but there was still a long way to go. Theo could only put weight on his injured leg for a step or two before the pain struck back.

The silver lining was that the pain was less intense each time. Thanks to adhering to his exercise regimen with clockwork precision, he could already discern more dexterity, and range of motion. He was well on the way to recovery. Another step closer to spending the rest of his life with Lady Beatrice.

Theo forced himself not to grimace at the

thought. He had no desire to speed along his impending marriage. Perhaps that was why he was standing in the corridor with one ear cocked for the sound of a brass knocker.

He almost tumbled from his crutches when Virginia walked around the corner carrying her wicker basket.

"You didn't knock," he blurted out, mortified at having been caught waiting like a puppy. "Did you bring ice cream this time, or some other misbegotten creature to add to my growing collection?"

"The color of the plumage does not determine the worth of the bird." She set the basket down just inside the front parlor. "Walk this way so I can see how you're doing."

When he reached her, Virginia dropped to a crouch and ran her hands over his leg. "Does it hurt when I touch it?"

His brain emptied of all logic every time she touched him anywhere.

"No," he managed.

She frowned. "It feels swollen."

"I rarely need the ice," he assured her.

To anyone else, he would not have admitted any pain or weakness. Virginia was different. From the moment he'd realized she required direct cues, he had found himself adapting to ensure she understood what he thought, how he felt.

It was not honesty that was new to him, but the vulnerability that came with it. Other people might have known him for longer, but she was seeing sides of him he had never shown to anyone.

He swept into the parlor as elegantly as a military officer on crutches could do and dropped himself into a chair near the fire.

"Join me," he said as he lowered his crutches to the floor. "Are you peckish?"

"I hope you are." She brought her basket into the room, then hesitated. "Do you like these visits?"

"Yes," he admitted gruffly.

Her eyes met his. "Me, too."

He was pleased by her admission. She had also begun meeting his gaze more often. Theo wasn't certain if it was because she was changing or because he was.

"You have pretty eyes," he said before he could stop himself. Curse his tongue. It was not the sort of comment one made to someone with whom one was trying to maintain a platonic relationship.

Her cheeks flushed pink. "Everything about you is handsome."

Definitely not the icy response required to keep the heat between them at bay.

"Thank you for having the staff prepare my favorite foods," he said gruffly. Surely that was a safer topic. "What's in the basket?"

She opened the lid with a little smile. "Ice cream."

He shot up straight, stomach growling in eager anticipation. He held out his hand. "You were right. I am indeed peckish."

"Good." She pulled a small covered dish and a spoon from the basket but handed him only the spoon.

He glanced around the room. "Shall we move to the tea table?"

Rather than respond, she carried his dish of ice cream to the furthest corner of the parlor and set it down behind one of Azureford's decorative folding screens.

"There you go," she said, as if her action made sense.

"There I go what?" he asked. "Searching for hidden ice cream? I know where it is. I saw you put it behind the folding screen."

"Go fetch it."

"Go…" He stared at her. "What did you just say to me?"

"The mother bird brings worms to her chicks so that one day, they may learn to hunt for themselves."

"You want me to hunt a bowl of ice cream?"

She nodded. "It's good for you. You rely too much on your crutches. They are not your mama bird."

With a sigh, Theo snatched his crutches up from the floor and hauled himself to his feet. "I'm not doing this for you. I'm doing it because I like ice cream."

He made it across the room to the folding screen without issue, then realized kneeling to pick up the bowl would require some ingenuity. There would be no way to do so in a graceful manner. Perhaps that was why she had placed the ice cream behind the screen. She had anticipated his reluctance for her to witness his ungainly first attempt.

He switched both crutches to one side and crouched with his good knee. The ice cream awaited, as promised. Unfortunately, the bowl barely contained a single spoonful.

"Did you eat this on the way over?" he called out.

"It's all for you," she replied.

"All of it?" he asked sarcastically. "The entire spoonful?"

She didn't answer.

He scooped the single creamy spoonful into his mouth and tried to savor it as long as possible. Because no one could see him, he tipped the bowl to his mouth and tried to scrape the last few sugary sweet drops before giving up and rising back to his feet.

He stepped out from behind the folding screen. "I fell for your dastardly trick. Walked all this way, only for—"

She was not where he had left her. Virginia was now on the opposite side of the room, balancing a small bowl on the back of the Duke of Azureford's plush settee.

"If that falls," Theo warned her, "the fabric will be ruined."

"Come fetch it, then." Virginia walked away from the sofa without a backward glance.

Theo glared at her, then glared at the settee and its precarious bowl of ice cream.

"I'm not doing this for you," he told her. "I'm preventing a crime against expensive satin."

She didn't answer.

This time, he could see it was because she was trying not to smile.

Minx.

He arranged the crutches beneath his arms and deposited the empty previous bowl on the closest tea table before continuing on to the sofa.

When he arrived, he realized the difficulty of the new task. He could not crouch, as he had done before. Nor could he lean the crutches against the sofa without toppling the bowl from its perch. He could transfer both crutches to one side, as he had done before, but he would have to count on the support of both his legs in order to rescue the bowl before it fell.

He turned to face her. "Are you naturally this diabolical, or—"

*Naturally this diabolical.*

She was across the room again, this time standing on her tiptoes to place a third bowl of ice cream high atop the Duke of Azureford's drawing room clock.

"What do you think you're doing?" he demanded.

"You like ice cream and need to stretch. This is the game."

He scowled at her. "It's a terrible game."

She peeked inside the wicker basket and made a sorrowful expression. "Do you want to stop playing?"

"Damn it," he muttered, and turned back to the sofa. "I'm not doing this for you—"

"You are doing it for yourself," she finished. "For your knee, and for regaining your confidence. The chair was your first crutch, and these are the new ones. The goal is to rely on them less, not more. You can do this."

"I know I can," he snapped without turning around.

He knew no such thing. Any second now, he was about to splatter half-melted ice cream all over the Duke of Azureford's furniture. Right before tumbling arse-over-teakettle himself.

From the corner of his eye, a stealthy black shadow crept into the parlor.

"No," Theo told the cat firmly. "Do not jump on the sofa. We'll both be wearing the ice cream."

Duke lowered his shoulders and arched his hips in preparation to pounce.

Theo's hand shot out and snatched the dish from the back of the settee seconds before the cat landed in the same spot.

Wood clattered against the Axminster carpet as his forgotten crutch crashed to the floor.

"This is your fault," he informed the cat, then turned to Virginia. "Yours, too."

Her eyes sparkled. "Hurry. Your competition just caught wind of the dish atop the clock."

Theo scooped the single bite of ice cream into his mouth, then bent to retrieve his fallen crutch.

He could not yet put his full weight on his wounded knee, but Virginia was correct that he had been using the crutches as extra legs instead of strengthening the ones he had.

She was also right that if Theo didn't do something soon, Duke would be first to the next bowl of ice cream.

He half-walked, half-swung himself across the parlor with more speed than he ever dreamed. Theo already shared a guestroom with that wretched creature. He wasn't about to share his ice cream, too.

Once he rescued the treasure, he shot a dark look at Virginia. "I thought you said recovery was a march, not a race."

"Recovery is a march," she agreed as she carried her basket to the other side of the room. "Ice cream is a race."

There was no way Theo was going to beat the cat that far... Unless he did something about it.

Foregoing the spoon, Theo tipped the bowl of melting ice cream to his mouth and swallowed the tiny serving. He slid the dish off the carpet and tapped his fingers against the hardwood floor to catch the cat's attention.

Duke glanced over his shoulder in boredom, then kept advancing toward the new bowl.

"You know you want it," Theo cajoled. *"Duke, Duke, Duke."*

The one word the beast could not resist.

With obvious irritation, the cat gave up its hunt for the fresh bowl of ice cream in order to race over and hiss.

Before the beast could run off, Theo scooted the dish beneath his chin.

Duke stopped baring his teeth at once and lowered his tongue into the bowl.

Victorious, Theo glanced over at Virginia.

She was not even trying to hide her laughter.

"Wars are won with brains, not brawn," he informed her as he swung past to retrieve his prize.

By the time the last of the ice cream had been consumed, Theo and Virginia were both giggling like children as they collapsed into side-by-side wingback chairs.

"That wasn't ice cream," he growled. "It was runny, melted sweet milk."

"Get faster," she replied unrepentantly. "I didn't hear Duke complain."

The beast opened one eye from his comfortable position curled before the fire, too sated to bother hissing in response to his name.

"Do you miss him?" Theo asked Virginia.

"I miss everything I love and no longer have." Her wistful gaze lowered to the cat at their feet. "Does he bring you comfort?"

Theo was fairly certain "comfort" was not the right term. "Did you lose someone you loved?"

"All of them," she said matter-of-factly. "And then I found new things to love."

"Like Duke?"

This time, the cat didn't even open an eye.

"I love all of Christmas," she said simply. "My friends, the nature that surrounds us, the castle."

He shook his head. "You can't love an inanimate object."

"I can." She lifted her chin. "I love the sharp scent of pine beneath the winter chill. I love the crunch of snow beneath my boots. I love the squeak in your front door."

"It's not mine," he murmured. "Take it up with Azureford."

"I love the library—"

"Books… come from trees that used to be animate, I suppose," he said with a straight face. "I'll allow it."

"I love that you arch your left eyebrow when I'm meant to take you seriously, and your right when I am not." Her lips curved. "And I love that I figured that out on my own."

Theo became uncomfortably aware of his eyebrows.

"I never jest," he told her solemnly.

"Then why does your right brow arch whenever you mention everyone else's expectations?"

"Everyone who?" he asked. "I don't care about anyone's opinion."

Except Virginia's. He realized he very much cared and did not wish for her to find him lacking.

She lifted a shoulder. "Lady Beatrice, your father…"

He scowled at her. "I thought you were rubbish at ferreting out people's feelings."

"I've been practicing with you for weeks." Her cheeks turned pink. "And I wasn't one hundred percent certain until you confirmed my suspicions just now."

"There are people who have known me for nine-and-twenty years who have not figured out as much as you have done in less than a month."

"Perhaps I try harder," she said softly.

He was not entirely certain he liked the idea that she could see deeper inside him than anyone had ever glimpsed before.

"Do you want to marry Lady Beatrice?" Virginia asked.

"No," he admitted. "But I will."

"Does she want to marry you?"

"No," he said. "She wants to marry a war hero. What she'll get is me." His shoulders tensed. "Our fathers agreed on this arrangement the day she was born. If I refuse, my father will disown me."

A darkness flickered in her eyes. "He can't disown a son. Sons are more important than daughters."

"To some fathers," Theo agreed. "For now, I am locked in an excruciating, never-ending apprenticeship. I cannot advance without proving my worth and am never given the opportunity to try."

"What is left to prove?" Virginia asked. "If your father is the only person who can't see your value, the fault lies not with you but with his willful blindness."

She didn't understand because she didn't know his father was a marquess… and the most exacting man of Theo's acquaintance. Even if pleasing his father was impossible, Theo still longed to be seen as an equal. To work side-by-side.

"My father," he said at last, "won't let go of the reins for a single moment. He controls everything and everyone in his life with ruthless precision."

"Birds of a feather," Virginia said. "You seem to have inherited your father's need for control."

He glared at her. "I am nothing like my father."

"Every ripple is unique, and exactly like those that came before." She pursed her lips. "Do you know the difference between the greater and lesser white-toothed shrew?"

"The greater white-toothed shrew is slightly larger, and its teeth are unpigmented." He pretended to stifle a yawn. "Who doesn't know that?"

"You didn't," she said in surprise. "One week ago."

Theo widened his eyes innocently. "That was before you loaned me an illustrated book on the topic."

"I didn't think you'd read it," she admitted.

He crossed his arms and gave her a good scowl. "I can read quite well. I've been making my way through Azureford's library."

Her eyes lit up. "Azureford has a library?"

He grinned. "Want to see it?"

She bounded out of her chair. "At once."

He fished his crutches from the floor and led her down the corridor to the duke's library.

Virginia's eyes shone as she took in the fireplace, the comfortable chairs, the towering rows of books, the proliferation of Roman statues on pedestals.

"It's marvelous," she breathed.

Theo wished he could show her his private library. Fewer statues of Juno and Cupid, but just as many books. He would love to see Virginia's face.

"Azureford must be a wonderful friend to allow you the use of his library."

"Azureford is a terrible friend. He left me at the mercy of his butler. I will have stern words for him when he returns."

Virginia frowned at the stacks. "All his books are arranged by size and color."

"That is the fashionable manner in which to display them. Libraries are meant to be aesthetically pleasing, not utilized."

She spun to face him.

"Aha," he said. "You missed my eyebrow. Now you will forever wonder whether I shelve my books in rainbow order or according to height."

"Neither," she said. "You've given yourself away by reading the one I loaned you. You appreciate books. Symmetry is lovely to gaze upon, but a ridiculous manner in which to organize a library. We should fix Azureford's."

Theo nearly choked. "We should what?"

"Organize it for him." Virginia lifted a palm toward the impeccable display. "Fiction with fiction, science with science, diaries with diaries."

"Azureford will hate it," Theo said. "It's exactly what he deserves. Where do we start?"

She grinned at him. "Follow my lead."

If Theo had found her beautiful before, Virginia was positively luminous when immersed in a task she was passionate about. Listening to her explain which categories should be grouped and which should never be conflated, which subjects were the most browsed in the castle library and therefore should be shelved as close to eye level as possible...

She was sweet and funny, clever and whimsical. The more he tried to hide his attraction, the harder she became to resist. It wasn't just that he wanted to taste her mouth in a kiss. He enjoyed her company, her unpredictability. The way she was completely and unapologetically Virginia.

When she came from around a bookcase staggering under the weight of an unwieldy stack of tomes, his protective instincts snapped into place.

"Put that down at once," he commanded.

"You're on crutches," she said as she lurched forward. "I've got it."

"You—" Theo shut his mouth.

She did have it. He just didn't like it. He wanted to be the one lifting heavy things for her.

"I'll sort these," he said gruffly as she sat the stack upon the closest table. "Lug as many back-breaking piles as you please."

A smile tugged at her lips. "I will."

They were halfway through their reorganization when a book of poetry whisked Theo's mind from the library altogether.

"What are you reading?" came a soft voice.

He jumped and shoved the book back onto a pile. "Nothing."

She picked it up. "Poetry?"

"Not everyone spends their days reading about the migratory patterns of African swallows."

She tilted her head. "You spend your days reading poetry?"

That wasn't what he had meant to admit at all.

"I have an affinity," he hedged.

She sat on the edge of the closest chair and motioned for him to do the same. "Tell me about it."

"Right now?" He glanced around. "We can't leave the library like... this."

"Trust me," she assured him. "It's not worse."

He sat. "I love poetry. I have a signed first edition copy of poems by Matilda Bethem. It's practically an extension of my soul. Is that what you want to know?"

She did not laugh at him or question why someone else's words could speak for him more eloquently than he could do so himself. She simply nodded as if books being the extension of one's soul was perfectly understandable.

He slid the slender volume from an inside pocket. He'd never shown it to anyone before. It truly felt like baring his soul. "My most prized possession."

"You had it with you when you went to war?"

"It never left my side." He tucked the poems back into their hiding spot and patted his chest. "If someone wished to stab me through the heart, they would have to do so through a hundred pages of poetry."

"That's beautiful," she said. "Of course it protected you."

Theo opened his mouth to argue the point, then realized she was right. He had been shot, trampled, scarred more places than not, but he would be fine. His heart had been safe behind its protective armor. The poems had done their job.

"Which one is your favorite?" she asked.

He considered. "The one that haunts me is called *The Heir*."

"What is it about?"

"A man who does what he must," Theo replied grimly. "Even forsaking the woman whose soul is entwined with his, because duty to one's title must always come first."

Her eyes widened. "It sounds ghastly."

Living it? Yes. The poem? No.

"It gives me peace to know no matter how bleak a situation one might find oneself in, beauty can always be made of it."

"Your face has not lost its beauty," she said softly. "How does your leg feel?"

"Almost good enough to dance," he promised. "If my knee could be trusted not to buckle beneath me."

"I'll see what I can do." She disappeared between the stacks.

Faster than he expected, the books were back on the shelves in the library in perfect working order. Not in the condition in which Azureford had left it, of course. But fiction with fiction, science with science, and all the poetry books at Theo's height.

He narrowed his eyes at her. "You did that?"

She blinked back at him innocently.

"*We* did this." She hesitated. "About dancing with Lady Beatrice…"

The words scraped like nails. Theo wanted nothing but Virginia on his mind for as long as possible. And he definitely did not want to think too hard about what that might mean.

"There may be a solution," she continued, "Even men without crutches aren't expected to dance every set."

He inclined his head in acknowledgment. "True."

She glanced at the clock in the corner. "I can spare another half an hour. What does a gentleman do when he's promised a set to a lady, but they've agreed not to dance?"

"Sneak her out to the balcony for a kiss?" Theo guessed hopefully.

She shook her head. "No balcony in here."

He blinked. Would a kiss have been an option if he'd said "between the stacks" instead?

"I've never stood up with a gentleman at a ball," she said. "For dancing or otherwise. You practice whatever is done in such situations, and at the same time I will learn what it is I am meant to do."

The idea of Virginia spending her time with other gentlemen—locked in a dance or otherwise —soured Theo's stomach.

"There's nothing to practice about spending half an hour with an honorable gentleman," he said. "What you need to learn is not to be taken advantage of by a boorish suitor."

"Perfect," she said. "I'll be me, and you can be my boorish suitor."

He grabbed her wrist and tugged her into the center of the room. When she complied, he glared at her. "That was the first test. You should not have come with me."

She frowned. "This is where you dragged me."

"I'm the boorish suitor," he reminded her. "Never let the boorish suitor drag you anywhere."

"What was I supposed to do?" she asked.

He pointed at his cheek. "Slap me."

"You're on crutches," she stammered.

"Don't slap me with one of my crutches. Just slap me."

She nodded as if taking a mental note. "Anytime a loutish gentleman tries to drag me somewhere I do not wish to go, I will slap them."

"Not just dragging," Theo said quickly. "If he makes lewd comments you dislike, touches you anywhere unwelcome, acts fresh or forward in any manner at all, slap him with your glove. If you're still wearing it, even better."

She nodded. "Understood."

"Next scenario," he said. "What do you do if a scoundrel tries to kiss you?"

She wrinkled her nose. "Mostly just stand there until he finishes."

He stared at her. "Does this happen often? I thought you'd never stood up with a man to dance before."

"Kissing isn't dancing," she pointed out. "Men needn't write their names upon one's card in order to steal a kiss."

"Writing their names upon your card is the very least that—" Theo clenched his fingers about his crutches and tried to slow his pulse. The blackguards in her past were not currently present for Theo to teach a lesson. He started again. "With the right man, you'll enjoy kissing. With the wrong one, slap him."

She made a face. "He was definitely the wrong one."

Theo tried to ignore the flash of relief at the realization that there had been only one such incident before. With Virginia, any of the usual assumptions were out the window. He wanted their first time to be perfect. Theo hadn't been this nervous about the thought of kissing a girl in twenty years. He didn't want her to look back on the memory and wrinkle her nose, but to sigh happily.

His heart skipped when he realized this meant he was thinking of their first kiss as a foregone conclusion. As inevitable as the tides, or the waxing of the moon.

"Here we go." He was glad they had the pretext of "boorish suitor" to protect them. If he kissed her as himself, in the way he truly wanted to... Who knew what would happen?

He closed the distance between them. Their toes were now touching. His lips could be on hers in a heartbeat.

"You're not wearing a fichu," he said. "I can look down your bodice from this angle."

She stared back up at him in silence.

"Slap me," he whispered. "That was an extremely impolite thing to say."

"You *can* see down my bodice from that angle," she said. "Do you like it?"

"I like your bosom from every angle," he growled. "That's not the point. The point is—"

Good Lord. He didn't even have to *act* to behave poorly.

Her lips curved. "I like how you look from every angle, too."

"Do not say things like that to a self-important cad," he warned her. "He'll think you mean them."

"I mean it with you." She peered up at him shyly, then glanced away. "I find you attractive."

Desire pulsed through Theo's blood. This lesson was not at all going the way he had planned.

"You are more than attractive." He could barely fight the craving to kiss her. It was more than the allure of plump red lips and long lashes over bright green eyes. It was Virginia. Everything about her was irresistible. "Scoundrels will be as captivated by you as I am. You must defend yourself."

"From what?"

"From this." He lowered his mouth to hers.

It was not a gentle kiss, as Theo might have intended, nor the carnal claiming that haunted his dreams. This was hard and firm and make-believe. Closed mouth to closed mouth. A common blackguard illustrating which one held the power. A kiss like this was not romance. It was a warning.

She didn't slap him.

As the moment stretched on, Theo found it increasingly difficult to keep up the arrogant, tightlipped pressure of a puffed-up lout. All Theo wanted to do was sink his fingers into Virginia's hair and kiss her the way she truly deserved to be kissed. He felt his mouth softening despite his best intentions. His lips parting of their own accord.

He jerked his head away before the kiss could turn into something he actually meant.

She immediately slapped him.

"Thank you," he said in relief. The torture had not been in vain. "Boorish scoundrels deserve retribution for stealing an unwilling kiss from a lady."

"I was willing," Virginia said. "I slapped you for stopping before it got better."

"Good God, woman." Theo staggered backward before he gave into temptation and did exactly that.

He absolutely, positively could not allow himself to touch her and mean it. Could he?

He was not yet spoken for. Nor was she. He was willing. So was she. They were alone. No one would ever know. He cast his eyes toward heaven. "Lord, please give me a sign."

"What?" Virginia stepped forward.

Theo backed away, lest he lose the last thread of control… and crashed directly into one of the many statues on pedestals. Something sharp pierced him as the figure wobbled off its base.

He tried to intercept it without dropping his crutches.

Virginia dashed forward and caught the statute before it could tumble to the floor. She placed the figure back on its pedestal and arranged it to face them.

Cupid.

Of course.

"You have got to be bamming me," he muttered.

"What?"

He'd asked for a sign, hadn't he? The Romans had answered. "Do you believe in Cupid?"

Her eyes widened. "Why?"

"His arrow just stabbed me in the back."

She held up her palm, where a spot of red marred the surface. "He got me, too."

"Then this is Fate," Theo growled, and slanted his mouth over hers.

This kiss was nothing like the first one. It was confident and real. Vulnerable and unapologetic. Now they both knew the truth. His only weakness was her. This kiss proved it.

Her lips were soft and yielding beneath his. Plump and inviting, as sweet and perfect as he had imagined. Yet he wanted more.

"Slap me," he whispered as he coaxed her lips to part.

"I will, when you do something I don't like," she murmured and opened her mouth to his.

Her kiss was exactly the nectar he had been dreaming of. Sweeter than the scent of roses. More dangerous than their thorns. This was a kiss he could lose himself in completely. He would not escape unscathed.

Each time Virginia relinquished power, she somehow also took it from him. He deepened the kiss. It did not give him the upper hand. She returned each kiss with the same abandon he had tried for so long to keep in check.

But it was a mirage. A wild, utopian fantasy they could indulge once, but never keep. He might not have signed a wedding contract, but his future was preordained. He would marry for his title, not his heart. Which meant he had no right to let Virginia think otherwise, even for a moment.

Reluctantly, he tore his mouth away and touched his forehead to hers.

"I would spend every minute of my time here

kissing you if I could," he forced himself to admit. "But that's all it could be."

She nodded. "I know."

He lifted his forehead and nudged up her chin with his knuckle to force her to meet his gaze. "You deserve more."

"I know," Virginia whispered. Without another word, she turned and left.

Theo sat down hard on the closest chair and shoved his crutches to the floor. There. He got his way and finally scared her off.

It didn't make him happy at all.

He rubbed his face with his hands. Being a marquess was like being a military officer, he reminded himself. One did as one must, not as one wished.

Chest tight, Theo pulled the book of poetry from its spot next to his heart and tossed it on to the closest shelf. It hadn't protected him today.

A black cloud slunk out from behind his chair and darted between the stacks of books.

Theo sighed. "You're a terrible chaperone, Duke."

At the sound of his name, the cat stalked out from its hiding place to bare its teeth in displeasure.

"Thank you, Your Grace," Theo said sarcastically.

Duke immediately rolled his paws skyward, twisted to scratch his back on the carpet, and gave a loud purr.

Theo blinked. "What in the—"

Duke stopped purring and stared at him.

Theo narrowed his eyes. *"Duke."*

The cat leaped onto its feet, claws out, and hissed.

This time, before it could run away, Theo immediately added, "Thank you, Your Grace."

Duke's claws vanished as he threw himself back to the floor, wriggling and purring in obvious pleasure.

Theo let out a surprised snort of laughter. The cat wasn't the prickly, antisocial creature he had seemed.

He had just been waiting to be treated like he mattered.

## CHAPTER 8

Virginia hesitated before the front step to the Duke of Azureford's cottage. No matter how hard she tried, she had not stopped thinking about the kiss she and Theodore had shared.

She did not blame him for trying to remind her of the walls between them. They were more insurmountable than he knew.

Even if he'd been willing to throw away his good standing and become the laughingstock of the *ton* by taking her as his bride or his mistress, Virginia was not. She would not risk her freedom.

Virginia was done being laughed at, looked down upon, *less than*. But although London was out of the question, she could choose to make the most of what time with Theodore remained.

She adjusted her basket, rolled back her shoulders, and knocked.

Swinton answered the door immediately. If he had watched her dither on the front step, he gave no sign. Instead, he motioned towards the corridor. "Front parlor today."

Virginia raised her brows. The front parlor was the furthest point from Theodore's guest quarters... and from the library where they had shared their kiss.

The curtains were drawn when she stepped into the room, giving the large parlor a cozy, sleepy feel. The only movement came from a fire dancing in the grate. The only sounds, the occasional crackling of a log.

And then she heard it.

A grin spread across her face as she rushed in the direction of Duke's familiar purr.

The little scamp was curled in Theodore's lap, stretching luxuriously whilst he enjoyed lazy scratches at his favorite spot behind his ear.

Theodore's wheeled chair was nowhere in sight. The wooden crutches lay on the floor, tucked within arm's reach of the plush armchair where he sat petting her cat.

"Traitor," Virginia said by way of greeting.

He nearly jumped out of his skin.

Laughing, Virginia took the seat opposite him. "Not you. *Duke.*"

At the sound of his name, Duke turned his head slightly and gave a halfhearted hiss. He was enjoying his scratches too much to put proper effort into the greeting.

Only when Theodore dropped his hand guiltily did Duke force himself from Theodore's lap and saunter to Virginia's feet.

"Watch this," Theodore said. "*Duke.*"

Duke turned and hissed.

Theodore cocked an eyebrow toward Virginia.

She shrugged. "I showed you that trick the day you met him."

"You didn't show me this one." Theodore turned back to Duke. "Thank you, Your Grace."

Duke flopped over onto his spine. Purring loudly, he rubbed his back against the carpet in random patterns.

Virginia's lips quirked.

Theodore pointed. "Did you know he would do that?"

"Of course. He is my cat."

"Why didn't you tell me?" Theodore demanded.

"Everyone knows 'Your Grace' is a proper way to address a duke," she reminded him, "and 'thank you' is common courtesy."

Theodore stared at her in consternation.

"Congratulations." Virginia tried not to let her grin show. "You have good breeding. Duke approves."

"I'll write a note to the papers to let them know."

"The three-bearded rockling's bright orange scales do not take his measure, but that of those around him." Virginia settled across from Theodore and narrowed her eyes. "You should consider a pet."

"I *had* a pet."

"You had one?" Virginia swallowed her dismay. "Is he… Did something happen?"

"Something happened." Theodore's jaw tightened. "I went to war. I could not abandon Coco to languish in my town house without me, and my father refused to allow a 'mongrel' on his property. I was forced to find her a new home."

Virginia's heart skipped in empathy. No wonder Theodore's bride needed to be perfect. His family would accept nothing less.

"When you return to London, will retrieving Coco be your first stop?"

"I don't know." Theodore ran a hand through his hair. "Checking on her, certainly. But I have been gone a long time. She was a puppy when I left, and now she is grown. She has a new family now."

"She didn't forget you." Virginia hoped he did not discern the tremble in her voice. "No one forgets their first family, no matter how they part."

"Good friends of mine took Coco in and have come to love her. What kind of man would I be if I took her from them?"

Virginia tried not to imagine how she would feel if Duke's first owners appeared out of nowhere and ripped him from her life. Theodore was right. Some things, once lost, could never be regained.

"Don't get any ideas with my cat," she said sternly. "Duke is a loan, not a gift. He won't be going to London."

"London weeps at His Grace's absence." Theodore gazed down at Duke curled between their feet. "I never thought I'd say this, but I'll miss the ill-tempered beast."

Virginia nodded. "That's exactly what he says about you."

Theodore's mouth curved. He gestured at her lap. "What's in the basket today?"

She patted the lid. "A special gift."

His eyes narrowed. "Ice cream?"

She shook her head. "Something even better."

"What could be better than ice cream?" he asked suspiciously.

"I'll show you." She opened the lid and pulled out the custom-built leg brace of walnut and metal she'd picked up at the le Duc smithy just that morning.

"Just so I'm clear," Theodore said. "Not better than ice cream."

She set down the basket and motioned for him to rise. "Up, up."

He scooped his crutches from the floor and launched to his feet. "Metal doesn't match my waistcoat."

She knelt before him to adjust the fit of the brace with its thick leather straps. "Does it hurt?"

"No," he said after a moment. "It's not touching my knee. What's it supposed to do?"

"Nothing, until you need it." She sat back. "The straps keep the brace affixed just above and below your knee. The hinges allow you to walk with normal motion. This mechanism here—" She touched two metal pieces. "—prevents your knee from buckling completely. Your leg won't fully bend while you are seated, but nor will it collapse beneath you if your goal is to remain upright."

"It's hideous." Theodore said. "Ask if it comes

in blue."

She grinned and held out her palm. "Walk."

His expression was dubious. "Without my crutches?"

"Take one, but try not to use it," she suggested. "Don't go fast. See how it feels."

He handed her one of his crutches and took a few hesitant steps. The new metal squeaked with each motion.

"Very good," she said approvingly.

"Very noticeable," he corrected. "I won't be caught dead with such a contraption in public."

"Then you must practice every day until you don't need it," she shot back.

"It's cold and heavy and displaces my balance." His gaze met hers. "But it helps. Thank you."

She bit her lip. "There might be a way you can return the favor."

He lifted his brows. "Name it."

Virginia took a deep breath. Now that her friends were scattering to the four winds, she would need to make new ones. Which meant mingling with her neighbors here in Christmas. Wild crushes were out of the question, but small dinner parties... Perhaps.

She'd turned down such invitations before, because attending would do more harm than good. She'd expose herself as the peculiar girl who didn't belong.

This was her opportunity to send the same old story in a new direction.

"You are good at High Society," she began slowly.

He cocked a brow. "You say that as if it were a dangerous sport."

"Isn't it?" Boxing and fencing would be safer. One chose a single opponent and the match never lasted for more than an hour. "Teach me what to do at a dinner party."

Theodore blinked. "A dinner party?"

Virginia nodded, not trusting herself to speak. If she explained her reasons, he might be the one to chuckle and think her peculiar.

With a single crutch under his arm, Theodore crossed to the closest bellpull and gave it a tug.

"How long will it take to prepare a four-course meal for two?" he asked the footman who answered the call.

"It needn't be real food," Virginia blurted out.

"Of course it does." Theodore nodded to the footman. "Send the first course to the dining room as soon as it's ready. We'll start with a glass of wine."

"At once." The footman dashed from the room.

Theodore turned to Virginia. "Would you do me the honor of allowing me to accompany you, Miss Underwood?"

She hurried to the side without a crutch, careful not to touch him.

"Take my arm," he whispered.

"I'll unbalance you," she whispered back.

His dark gaze heated her to her toes. "We'll find a way to manage."

She curved her fingers lightly about his arm. It was not the first time Society's rules dictated she take a man's elbow, but it was the first time she'd wanted to. The dark blue superfine of his jacket felt strange and inviting beneath her fingers.

They exited the front parlor at a slow, even pace, careful not to bump the walls or each other. When they reached the dining room, only the heads of the long table were set. Theodore had a footman move the place settings to the middle of the table, across from each other.

"We are not hosting," he explained without forcing her to ask. "We are attending. If you need to host a party, we can practice that scenario tomorrow."

"I will never host a party." The words came out more vehement than Virginia had intended.

"Then this will do." Theodore led her to a chair and did not take his until she was seated. "Now, when we look at our place settings, we see multiple forks and multiple spoons. The outermost silverware—"

"I know which fork does what," Virginia said. "I've eaten food before."

His brows rose. "My apologies. I did not realize the castle dining rooms were formal."

They were not. Virginia's parents had instructed their children in the proper use of silverware from the moment they were old enough to lift a fork. Mistakes were not tolerated.

"Perhaps we should start with the differences," Theodore began anew. "Does the castle observe precise dining hours?"

She shook her head.

"Very well. A formal dinner party differentiates itself from more casual dining customs before any of the party has taken their seats. A strict order of precedence is observed, meaning the first to the table is always—"

"I know about precedence," Virginia said. She could quote her mother's lectures from memory. "I know about controlling invitations to maintain proper numbers, seating arrangements that alternate men and women, not using one's gloves at the dinner table."

Theodore leaned back. "What exactly do you need me to teach you?"

"What to *say*." The back of her throat grew thick. "What to do. How to be."

Every day that she'd lived here in Christmas, she had longed to take part in the year-round holiday fun. Her fear of ruining the moment for others, of being overwhelmed by her senses, of not knowing *how* to take part had kept her from trying. She yearned for that to change.

He gazed at her for a long moment. "I gather you're not referring to the manners one might discover in a book on comportment."

She shook her head. If only it were that simple. "I've read all of those. Primogeniture, politesse, mind one's parents, never go outside without a bonnet. But the rules that seem to matter most are the unspoken ones no one bothers to teach."

"Have an example?"

"Make eye contact even when you don't want to," she said after a moment. "Stay within a socially acceptable distance that changes according to each person's preferences. Say 'how droll' to the host even when he isn't."

The corners of his eyes crinkled. "You're absolutely right. Those *are* the rules, and I've never heard them taught in any school."

"Can you help?" she asked.

"I can try." His expression turned serious. "Those are the sorts of issues one notices when things don't go as expected, rather than a list of prohibited behaviors I could write down for you to memorize."

"That's always the problem." She tried to swallow her frustration.

"We'll find a way," Theodore said. "Don't give up on me yet."

A footman arrived with the first course. Virginia was pleased to see tonight's soup was chestnut.

Theodore sent her a considering gaze. "I suppose there's no need to explain who does the serving and how second helpings are handled?"

No. Virginia could serve the king himself. She just wouldn't know what to say to him.

"If the topic of conversation appears to be the weather," she began haltingly, "and, after having discussed the current climactic conditions exhaustively, the entire party turns to me as if expecting my input but without having asked a direct question... What do I say?"

Theodore arched a brow. "This doesn't sound like a hypothetical question."

She shook her head. "It's every single outing with strangers."

"Go out with friends instead," he suggested with a smile.

She didn't smile back. It was exactly the problem.

"Here is a foolproof trick." Theodore leaned forward. "Repeat the hostess. Just say, 'I agree with Queen Turkey-tiara. Rain *does* seem to make the road wet.'"

She giggled. "But what if Queen Turkey-tiara has the opinions of a featherwit?"

"It doesn't matter. No one can criticize you without offending the host. They wouldn't dare." He sat back. "Works every time."

While Virginia considered Theodore's words, a footman arrived with the next course.

She bit her lip. "What do I do if one of the ladies across from me makes rude expressions in my direction?"

"Nothing," Theodore said at once. "If you don't outrank her, act like you can't see her. It will drive her mad."

"What do I do if the gentleman next to me passes wind?"

"Audible or olfactory?" he inquired politely.

"Give me both scenarios."

He burst out laughing. "What kind of dinner parties have you attended?"

"That hasn't happened," she admitted. "But it could."

"Help me." Theo stabbed his fork into the vegetables and affected a horror-struck expression. "If the boiled asparagus is too limp to stay on my fork, what do I do?"

She kicked him under the table.

"Careful," he said. "You'll injure my good knee."

"If I'm roasting chestnuts on an open fire and the gentleman next to me loses his handkerchief into the flames, what do I do?" she asked.

He leaned forward. "If a caroler's high-pitched falsetto cracks the lenses of my spectacles, what do I do?"

"If, whilst playing charades, I'm meant to imitate the Prince Regent singlehandedly consuming the buffet at Carlton House, what do I do?" she countered.

Theodore widened his eyes. "If the woman across from me doesn't realize she's already the perfect dinner partner just as she is, what do I do?"

Virginia's cheeks flushed with pleasure. She wasn't the perfect one. *He* was. Or perhaps two imperfect people could be perfect together.

As soon as the supper dishes were cleared, a footman swept into the dining room bearing a silver tray. "Pupton of apples."

Theodore's face lit up.

Virginia's feelings were more bittersweet. There was nothing she loved more than dessert. But there was nothing she hated more than knowing this course meant their impromptu dinner party was coming to a close.

"If you're not going to eat your dessert," Theodore said, "I will do the honorable thing and personally dispose of both portions."

She stuck her fork in the corner of his dish and lifted the morsel of baked apples to her mouth. "Mmm."

He reached across with his fork to do the same.

She lifted her dish close to her chest to keep it out of his reach.

"Unfair," he said. "If I held a pupton that close to my chest, the majority would end up in my neckcloth."

"I've lost several crumbs down my bodice," she admitted. "You don't want them."

"That is an erroneous assumption." The heat from his dark gaze melted her to her core. "If my ungainly hobble wouldn't ruin the moment, I'd stalk to your side of the table and steal a kiss for my dessert."

Heart pounding, she set down her plate. "Stand up. I'll meet you halfway."

Theodore scrambled to his feet at once.

Virginia placed her hands atop the table and leaned as far forward as she could.

He glanced down at her bosom. "Should I rescue those crumbs, or—"

She lifted her gaze to his. "You should kiss me."

"I thought you'd never ask."

When his mouth touched hers, the world about them fell away. He tasted like cinnamon sugar apples and warm mulled wine and cozy winter nights. It was impossible not to wish every meal she took could end just like this.

The width of the table prevented them from falling into each other's embrace. They could lock nothing but mouths, touch nothing but tongues. It was more than enough. He didn't just make her feel visible. He made her feel like she mattered. Like nothing was more important than their mouths joined in a kiss.

She had to remind herself that none of this was real. A romance could never be. The only reason either one of them indulged the irresistible force drawing them together was because the night was wrapped in make-believe. The pretend dinner party. His cloak of anonymity.

Soon enough, this holiday would end.

Virginia didn't want to think about any of that. She wanted to pretend his kisses would belong to her forever. That when Theodore's legs were strong again, he would use them to sweep her off her feet, not to waltz with Lady Beatrice at their wedding. Virginia needed to stay strong.

Theodore could have her kisses. But she could not let him have her heart.

A throat cleared in the doorway.

Virginia and Theodore jerked apart to see Swinton gazing at them with an impassive expression. "Dinner was to your liking?"

Too much so.

"I have to go." Virginia dashed from the table, squeezed past Swinton, and hurried back out into the snow before her ardor could cause her to make even bigger mistakes.

"Virginia!" called a voice. "*Virginia!*"

She slowed. That wasn't Theodore. It was—

"Penelope?" she asked in bewilderment.

Her friend stood at her open door and motioned Virginia to join her. "Get inside!"

Virginia wrapped her arms about her chest and dashed up the walk.

"Why are you walking around in this weather without a pelisse?" Penelope demanded.

*Her coat.* Virginia groaned. She hadn't just left that behind; she'd left everything. Her hat, her gloves, her basket.

"It seemed warmer when I left," she mumbled. A lot warmer.

"I'll loan you one of mine," Penelope said. "No arguments."

Virginia frowned. "I thought you had already left for London."

"Not yet." Penelope's eyes shone. "We were in Bristol visiting the best glassmakers in the country."

Virginia presumed this had something to do with one of Penelope's perfumes. She was a lady chemist, and one of the smartest women Virginia knew. Her debut cologne-water, *Duke*, had taken England by storm. So had Penelope. She was the opposite of Virginia in every way.

Penelope clasped her hands together and grinned. "I don't know what I would do without you."

Virginia blinked. "Without… me?"

"Your timely words to Nicholas were not only the inspiration for his marriage proposal." Penelope lifted two glass bottles from a wooden crate upon the floor. "You also inspired the new packaging for *Duke* and *Duchess*."

In amazement, Virginia accepted the fist-sized perfume bottles. "Turtledoves?"

"Turtledoves." Penelope beamed at her. "Glassblowers are hard at work copying Nick's designs, my perfumes are more popular than ever… The surge in sales is all thanks to you. That's why we just signed a trust giving you one percent of dividends earned in perpetuity."

"It was just a comment," Virginia stammered. "I'm not a chemist or an artist. 'Turtledoves' were just... words."

"Words matter, and no one is more creative with them than you." Penelope touched Virginia's shoulder. "Your ideas are important. *You* are important."

Virginia stared at the interlocking glass perfume bottles in awe. One percent of dividends earned in perpetuity. Because she'd had an idea that mattered.

"I want to open an animal sanatorium," she blurted out.

"You should," Penelope said without hesitation. "You are incredible with animals."

"The castle just hired an expert veterinarian," Virginia confessed. "He arrived today. He doesn't care about my opinions."

Penelope rolled her eyes. "That's because he's the sort of man who thinks women can't be experts. Ignore him."

Virginia's shoulders hunched. "He's had formal schooling at university. Years of paid experience."

"And now he's working in a two-bird aviary," Penelope pointed out. "I'm not impressed."

"Fifteen birds," Virginia admitted. "I donated my collection."

"Then he owes more to you than you do to him." Penelope lifted her chin. "If you have a dream, you should follow it."

# CHAPTER 9

irginia was at her writing desk drawing plans for her sanatorium when a knock came on her chamber door. She opened it to reveal a footman bearing a familiar wicker basket.

He held out the basket. "Mr. T requests the pleasure of your company at once."

"I'll think about it." Virginia accepted the basket.

It was heavier than usual. When the footman left, she set the basket atop her bed and opened the lid. One by one, she placed its contents in a line.

Her bonnet. Her winter gloves. Her favorite pelisse. A folded scrap of paper.

She unfolded the paper. The sparse handwriting inside read only:

*Come peckish.*

Her heart gave a dangerous flutter. After having fled from their make-believe dinner party the night before, Virginia hadn't been certain when she would be ready to face Theodore again. Or if he would even want to see her.

This answered one of the questions.

She slid on her pelisse and gloves and tied on her bonnet. Her heart lightened. The walk down to Azureford's cottage seemed to take half the time as usual.

When she rapped the knocker, Swinton led her not into one of the various drawing rooms, but straight through the cottage to the rear exit.

Were they headed to the outbuilding?

Virginia frowned. She'd come peckish, but would *not* be eating the partridge.

Swinton turned her not toward the outbuilding, but to a wooden-latticed belvedere on the other side. Thick woolen blankets covered most of the interior. Upon its cozy surface sat two wooden crutches, one handsome viscount, and a picnic basket.

"I know what you're thinking," Theodore said. "And no, we cannot be trusted to behave ourselves inside."

Virginia glanced around at the thick copse of evergreens buffeting the rear garden in total seclusion, then returned her questioning gaze to Theodore.

"It's cold," he said. "That helps more than you think."

Cold, but not freezing. She stepped closer.

Snow still covered the trees and grass, but the air was calm and dry.

"I hope you'll forgive me if I don't rise to greet you," he said. "I believe I found the most awkward way possible to lower my backside to the blanket and I'd like to spare you from having the image in your head."

"I don't mind awkward." She settled across from him. "What's in the basket?"

He clasped his hands to his chest and affected a joyous expression. "I've made metal braces for your elbows, knees, and ankles."

She burst out laughing. "You did not, beast. Knowing you, that's a basket full of ice cream."

He did not respond.

"It is a basket full of ice cream?" she asked in disbelief. "For a winter picnic?"

"Technically, it's April," he reminded her. "April is definitely ice cream weather."

He opened the lid to the basket and began to place dishes of ice cream atop the blanket.

"If you insist on normalcy," he said, "there may also be cheese, bread, and fruit somewhere inside the basket."

"I've never once been normal," she assured him, and picked up a dish of ice cream.

Theo's eyes sparkled with approval.

It didn't take them long to have done with their sweet, creamy feast.

He stacked the dishes inside the basket and moved it aside in order to lie back with his hands laced behind his head.

Virginia did the same, but in the opposite direction. She could see him if she lifted her head, but this way she could keep her gaze on the clouds overhead rather than the handsome man at her side.

"Do you like Christmas?" she asked after a moment.

"The town?" Theodore paused, as if considering his response. "I like you. I haven't seen the town. In a sense, being anonymous here is harder than being away at war."

She frowned. "In what way?"

"On the front lines, we still received letters and news of home." His eyebrows drew together. "It's unsettling not to have contact."

Virginia could not disagree more. She thanked her stars every day that no one from London ever tried to contact her. She was *not* going back to that asylum.

Another terrible thought slammed into her. What if her parents numbered among Theodore's acquaintances when he returned to London? What if he inquired about her, and they had nothing nice to say, other than getting rid of her being the best thing they could ever have done?

"I don't mind the lack of contact," she said. "No one cares what I do. I can only be tolerated for short periods."

"That is a horrible thing to say." He jerked up on one elbow. "Why the devil would you think that?"

"It might have taken even longer to figure out, had so many helpful individuals not seen fit to say

138

so directly. Lord Munroe, Lady Voss, my mother…"

"Wait. What?" Theodore shot up straight, his jaw hanging open. "Who are your parents?"

"You don't know them," Virginia said, and prayed it was true. "They've only a baronetcy to their name."

"Lady Underwood and Sir Hubert are your parents?" he said in disbelief. "*Horrid* ones, from the sound of it."

Virginia closed her eyes in mortification. "You know them."

"I haven't had the pleasure. But I recall the names from Debrett's Peerage and Baronetage. Does your family live with you in the castle?"

She shook her head. "They live in London. I live in the castle."

He stared at her. "How does something like that happen?"

His question seemed to stretch out between them, a razor-sharp whip of words and implication, capable of snapping back to break her in two.

Virginia kept her eyes closed and concentrated on the evergreens rustling in the breeze. She would not lie to Theodore. But to answer meant sharing secrets she guarded for a reason. If her own family found her unlovable and not worth their attention, Theodore might feel the same.

But she couldn't keep him anyway, Virginia reminded herself. This was why. He might as well know the truth.

"It's not their fault," she said at last. The wind stole each word; made it colder. "Not completely.

They have a little money but no sons. The baronetcy and our entailed home will go elsewhere, leaving my mother and sisters homeless and penniless. Making it essential to marry well, starting with the eldest daughter." Her throat stung. "It was my responsibility to wed quickly and upwardly so that my younger sisters could do the same."

Even with her eyes closed, she could feel Theodore staring at her.

"You had a Season," he said in growing understanding.

She nodded. "Part of one. It didn't go well. Since my parents couldn't be rid of me that way, they had to find another."

"What other way?" Theodore demanded.

Virginia swallowed the old hurt. "It's natural. All baby chicks must be thrust from the nest when it's time to fly."

"When they are *ready* to fly," he corrected. "Good bird-parents don't banish their baby chick to a castle on the opposite side of England because she had a bad first Season."

"They didn't." Virginia's voice cracked. "They sent me to a lunacy asylum on the other side of that forest."

"They what?" Theodore's growl was low and deadly.

A breeze blew through the lattice. Its chill was nothing compared to the cold inside. "An unmarriageable daughter is of no use to anyone. My reputation no longer mattered."

"What about your future?" he growled. "Your life?"

"I couldn't have one." She opened her eyes, but did not look at him. "Not when I stood in everyone else's way. The eldest must marry first. My parents told everyone I had contracted a strange disease and was being looked after in some hospital."

"But there was no strange disease." His nostrils flared. "And no hospital."

"Maybe there was. Maybe I'm the strange disease. I've been peculiar since birth, and my parents could not wait to wash their hands of me." Virginia's heart clenched. Telling the story had not made it easier.

"Why up here?" Theodore asked as the wind ruffled his hair. "This distance requires weeks of travel every time they visit you."

"It would," she agreed. "If they had visited. My parents needed me as far away as possible. It would have been risky to send me someplace close by, like Ticehurst or Bedlam. Too many people visit for the great sport of laughing, mocking, and poking sticks at inmates. They didn't want their friends to recognize me."

His hand brushed her cheek. "You do realize that this is not an acceptable way to treat one's child?"

"Have you ever been in a madhouse?" she asked bleakly. "They're crowded. Every one of the inmates is someone's child."

He pulled her into his arms and held her close.

"It's fine," she said hoarsely, determined not to

cry. It had never helped before. "All sorts of animals abandon their young. Rabbits, house sparrows, cuckoos…"

"To the devil with that," Theodore said. "And to the devil with your family. You're not a house sparrow. No one can take care of themselves in a madhouse."

"I learned that the hard way," she whispered. "I tried to run away every single day. It took three years to finally happen."

He shivered. "I don't blame you for coming here instead of going to London."

"I didn't mean to do that, either," she admitted.

The night she'd escaped, Virginia had been terrified. Leaving the asylum was the first decision she'd made for herself. She was unprepared for the weather, for the loneliness, for the unexpected surprise of kind strangers.

A caravan of tourists was heading further north to take their holiday in a village called Christmas. They had assumed her carriage had broken down and offered her passage. Virginia had swallowed her terror and accepted.

She kept her mouth shut the entire journey. She could not risk being odd or funny or peculiar. Any time she was too wrong, people tossed her aside like rubbish. But Christmas hadn't. It had welcomed her as if it had been waiting for her right here Virginia's entire life.

Mr. Marlowe not only gave her the run of the castle and a room of her own, but a generous allowance. It wasn't just that Virginia didn't want for anything. For the first time, she awoke each morning without fear.

"The best part about Christmas is that here, I can live as I am. There are no expectations except my own. It's the most freedom I've ever had." Her voice shook. "I wouldn't give it up for anything."

"Only a blackguard would ask you to." His lips twisted. "I'm surprised your parents allowed you to stay."

She lifted a shoulder. "They don't know I'm out of the madhouse."

He stared at her. "How long have you lived here?"

Even the wind was quiet in anticipation of her response.

"Six years," Virginia admitted in a small voice. She could practically see him do the sums.

"Your family dropped you off at a lunacy asylum nine years ago and haven't noticed you are not still there?"

"No one's come looking for me." Her cheeks burned at the admission that no one missed her. "I've stopped worrying I'll be sent back."

"Maybe they did have a change of heart," Theodore suggested after a moment, his tone hopeful. "Maybe they came to visit, couldn't find you, and have been desperately searching for you ever since."

"I asked Mr. Marlowe to let me know if any notices were ever posted in the papers. If my parents were looking for me. None ever came. Eventually, I stopped asking about the past and started over instead. At first, I had nothing. Now I do."

She gave a wobbly smile. "I have Duke, I have my friends, I have my afternoon constitutionals…"

His gaze was unreadable. "I'm not certain 'afternoon constitutional' is a possession."

"They are the most precious possessions I own." She swallowed. "I walk outside every day regardless of the weather because I *can*. Because it proves I'm free."

"I stand corrected." He pressed a kiss to the top of her head and cuddled her close. "There is no greater possession than freedom."

"Nobody knows," she whispered. "Except you. I didn't tell anyone but Mr. Marlowe about the asylum, and I told no one at all about London. I didn't want my friends here to look at me the same way people had back there. Wondering what made me so backwards. Why I couldn't be fixed."

"You don't need to be fixed," he said fiercely. "There is nothing wrong with you. You are perfect just as you are."

Virginia didn't answer. There was no point. The lie was pretty, but they both knew it wasn't true. It was the reason they could never be together.

He released her from his embrace and struggled to his feet. "Stand up."

Her mouth went dry. This was it. The moment when he sent her from his home, never to speak to her again. "What are you going to do?"

He held out his hand. "What are *we* going to do."

She rose on shaky legs. "What are *we* doing?"

He placed her hand on his shoulder. "We're

going to waltz. I want my first dance after years of battle to be with you."

Her heart leapt.

"I thought you wanted Lady Beatrice to be your first dance," she stammered.

"I haven't thought about her at all." His eyes were serious. "I'm hoping to dance with my cousin. It's her first season, and Hester is afraid she'll spend it without a single name upon her card."

Virginia's pulse skipped. "That's the news from London you've been missing?"

He nodded. "She's a sweet lass. She deserves all the dances she might wish. I must get healthy in order to stand up with Hester without embarrassing her. Other than my ruined face, of course."

"She won't be embarrassed." Virginia touched his cheek and smiled. "You don't need to be fixed, either."

She could not believe this moment was happening. She had confessed her darkest secret: that the only way she enriched anyone's life was by staying out of it. And his response had been to pull her into his embrace.

Their waltz was slow and halting. Virginia did not mind. She'd had to live most of her life in such a manner. This moment was magical.

She was dancing with the man of her dreams. Not in a crowded ballroom, filled with too many bodies and too much perfume and dripping candle wax, but outside, amid the natural beauty she so cherished.

Theodore's knee buckled. Virginia and the metal brace caught him before he fell.

"Shall we sit back down?" she asked.

"I'm not ready to let you out of my arms."

"Try this." She stepped closer, wrapping both arms above his shoulders and pressing her body to his for support.

"How am I supposed to lead you about like that?" he said gruffly.

"Don't," she said simply. "I'm not going anywhere."

He lowered his arms to encircle her waist.

Instead of the wide steps of a waltz, they rocked side to side, slowly, peacefully. Not to the insistent three-beat rhythm of an orchestra, but to the lazy afternoon breeze and the thumping of their hearts.

"This is not how waltzes work," he whispered into her ear.

"I know." She lay her face on his chest. "It's nicer."

Being with Theodore was easy. If he wanted something, he told her. If she did something unexpected, he went along. With him, she could be herself. He liked her just as she was, peculiarities and all. Was it any wonder she had fallen in love?

She stumbled at the realization.

He caught her.

"Shall I commission leg braces for you?" His low voice rumbled into her hair.

Not a leg brace. A metal box to hide her heart away and keep it safe. But she suspected it was far too late for armor. With Theodore, she had no defenses at all.

"Virginia?"

She forced herself to look up and meet his eyes.

His smile was victorious as he dipped his head to steal a quick kiss. "I like how you waltz."

"I like how you kiss," she answered, and immediately ducked her head, so he would not see the full truth on her face.

He liked her well enough up here in Christmas, far away from his peers. London was a different world. If she gave her heart to him, only for him to toss her away...

She would not be able to survive it a second time.

# CHAPTER 10

"*Come*," Theo commanded.

Duke opened his eyes, yawned, and closed them again.

"If you can learn to respond to your name and your honorific, you're clever enough to learn other words, too." In fact, Theo was willing to bet Virginia had taught the beast an entire vocabulary. He crossed his arms. "Come here, now."

Duke rolled to face the opposite direction.

Theo changed tactics. "Come hither, almighty cat-beast."

Duke let out a short purr that sounded suspiciously like a snicker.

Theo tried again. "O great and powerful—"

"You have a visitor," Swinton announced from right behind them.

Theo jumped, and winced when the action jarred his knee. He looked over the butler's shoulder and saw no one. "Where is she?"

"In the outbuilding."

Checking on the partridge? Theo frowned.

148

He'd given his word to care for it. Surely, she trusted him by now.

"And the surprise I have planned?" he asked.

"In the mews, awaiting your summons."

"Have a footman bring it up front."

Theo had been waiting all day for Virginia to arrive. He hurried down the corridor as fast as his leg brace and wounded knee would allow.

He caught her in the outbuilding just as she was stuffing the partridge inside a wicker basket.

"What are you doing with Dancer?"

She shut the lid. "Taking him back to the castle."

"I thought he was my responsibility now." Theo folded his arms over his chest. "Part of my afternoon constitutional."

She glanced up guiltily. "I may have neglected to mention that I don't own this bird."

He stared at her. "I've been playing nanny to a stolen partridge?"

"Borrowed," she assured him. "You were too injured to visit the aviary, so I promised to bring it to you."

"I thought you were being metaphorical."

"At the time, it made no difference. No one visited the aviary but me."

He arched his brows. "Has the prospect of viewing a dozen birds suddenly become all the rage in Christmas?"

"Loads of birds," Virginia corrected. "The new veterinarian arrived along with a sizable collection. Everyone in town has finally realized the aviary is worth visiting. You should see it."

Theo resisted glancing down at his leg brace or touching his fingertips to the scarred half of his face. "No need. The pleasure of Dancer's company was more than enough."

He plucked the basket from her hands and led her through the rear entrance toward the front of the cottage.

When they arrived at the entryway, he handed the basket to Swinton. "Can you please see this partridge anonymously returned to the castle aviary?"

To his credit, Swinton asked no questions. "I'll have it done."

"I could have taken him," Virginia said.

"And have them discover it was you who stole him?" Theo pointed out.

"They already dismissed me," she said with a shrug. "Besides, I would have returned him when no one else was present."

Of course. Theo winced. The last thing Virginia would do was voluntarily enter a loud, crowded chamber.

"While everyone else is at the castle," he told her, "I have something I think you might like."

She tilted her head. "What is it?"

"Christmas." He opened the front door.

There in front of the cottage was the sleigh he had rented for this occasion. Theo had paid the owner to take a day's holiday. One of Azureford's footmen held the reins instead.

"A sleigh ride?" Virginia said in wonder. "I've always wanted to try it."

Sleighs were a common sight in Christmas,

and typically brimmed with passengers. Theo remembered she had worried about being overwhelmed by too many sensations at once. Of the possibility of making a fool of herself in front of her neighbors.

"Just you and me," he promised. He held out his arm. "Shall we?"

She did not take his elbow.

"What if someone sees us?" she whispered. "*Together.*"

He did not have to parse her meaning. "You are worried about becoming accidentally compromised by me?"

"Aren't you?" she asked.

Fear hadn't crossed Theo's mind. He pushed the question away, rather than examine it too closely. "It's no different than a curricle ride in Hyde Park. Besides, we'll be bundled in scarves, hats, and outerwear. While everyone else is at the center of town, we'll meander through the evergreens along the edge. Just us, in an endless forest of snow-covered trees."

"It does sound Christmassy," Virginia admitted and lifted her hand to his arm. "I'm ready."

Once she was bundled in the center of the sleigh, he eased down beside her. It might surprise and perhaps embarrass her to know how proud Theo was of her courage.

Things that were easy for others were difficult for Virginia, yet she never ceased trying to conquer them. Practicing dinner parties, overcoming a fear of animals to become an accomplished healer, building a new life for herself when the one she should have had was ripped away.

A sleigh ride was the least he could offer her. He loved that she loved Christmas, and would make it his mission to give her as much of the holiday as he could.

He wrapped his arm about her. The horses and driver led them away from the cottage and down a narrow trail leading to the forest.

"Should we sing carols?" he asked. "Just you and me?"

"Perhaps another day. I like doing one new thing at a time." She nestled into his shoulder. "Right now, I am enjoying being with you."

Theo's heart thumped. He'd been enjoying every moment with her since the day they met. She gave him a reason to greet each day beyond London and war. She gave him peace.

He gazed at the slowly passing fields of snow-topped evergreens. The world was silent except for the soft sound of horse hooves upon the snow. The only scent in the crisp winter air was that of pine. Comforting warmth came from the woman cuddled next to him. He hoped she loved this moment half as much as he did.

The corner of his mouth twisted. She'd trusted him enough to share the most vulnerable parts of her past with him. It was time for him to come clean about his own identity. Even if it changed everything.

"I asked you to call me Theodore instead of Mr. T," he began slowly.

She nodded. "I remember."

"Obviously that is not my full name." He hesitated. "I am Lord Ormondton. A major and a viscount."

She nodded. "I know."

"You know?" He stared down at her. "Since when?"

"Since you had me post a letter to your father."

"I didn't say it was my father," he spluttered. "He is known as Lord Ramsbury."

"All my friends said that Ramsbury's son is a strong, clever, selfless, courageous hero." She peered up at him through her lashes. "No one fits that description better than you."

His heart gave a little flip and he held her closer. "It describes you just as well."

Her lips curved. "I am not Lord Ramsbury's son."

"Care to trade?"

"There are two kinds of family." Her voice lowered, and her gaze turned wistful. "The kind you are born with, and the one you make yourself."

Theo hoped he was someone she would choose to keep.

"Tell me about the marquessate," she said. "Is it large and complicated?"

"Large," he admitted. "But I've been memorizing every detail since I was old enough to toddle."

"Every detail?" She lifted her brows. "What kind of trees does it have?"

"Oak, elm, pine, juniper, plane trees, and several varieties of buckthorn." He gave her a placid smile. "Would you like to know the percentages per hectare?"

Her eyes sparkled. "Tell me about the fauna."

"Deer, squirrels, hares, hedgehogs, foxes, and grouse, to name a few." His chest warmed. "One of my favorite spots is the folly overlooking the pond. No one goes there but me. It's the perfect place to watch the sunrise or to see ducklings swim in a row after their mother."

"It does sound perfect," she murmured.

He wished he could take her with him.

"The marquessate belongs to my father, not me." He gave a rueful smile. "The best I have to offer is an elegant Mayfair town house."

"Does it have a pond in the center?"

He shook his head. "Fancy carpet."

She clucked her tongue. "Missed opportunity."

"Ducks might like my carpet," he protested. "I'm thinking of having some delivered. I'm an excellent bird nanny."

"You are an indulgent bird nanny," she corrected. "Don't think I missed how plump Dancer has become."

"I didn't know he was the castle partridge," Theo protested. "I thought he was a hard-luck partridge, scraping by on his last feather."

She lifted her chin. "Dancer has all his feathers."

Theo nodded slowly. "That should have been a clue."

Virginia patted his chest. "You're not ready to be a bird nanny."

He sighed. "I suppose I won't have time anyway. Once I inherit the marquessate, I'm to become an automaton like my father."

She wrinkled her nose. "Why don't you become Theodore?"

"I'm already Theodore."

"Exactly." Her gaze softened. "I don't see a reason for you to change."

"That's because you've never had the pleasure of one of my father's detailed and lengthy discourses on the topic," Theo said dryly.

"Disappointing," she said. "I'd assumed your father to be intelligent."

"He is intelligent," Theo said. "He is one of the most respected and powerful—"

Why was he arguing? He didn't have to prove himself or his credentials to Virginia. She had already accepted him exactly as he was.

It was a bewildering concept. Theo had spent his life living up to other people's standards. Virginia didn't give a hot fig what people like Theo's father thought. Perhaps in part because she literally couldn't tell, but more importantly, she had decided it was outside her control. People would think as they would.

The high regard that mattered the most to Theo was Virginia's. It would destroy him if the woman he loved lost her faith in—

God save him. He was in *love*.

His body froze in place. His pulse began to gallop as if a thousand enemy soldiers had surrounded him with muskets. Their shots came too late. He had fallen, damn it all. And it terrified him.

Theo had walked away from London. He'd been carried away from war. He did not want to lose Virginia.

What the devil was he going to do about it?

Lady Beatrice had been selected for him at birth, although their personalities had always been wrong for each other. He gazed down at Virginia. No one had ever felt more right.

Theo grimaced at the impending confrontation. He and Lady Beatrice weren't children anymore. They would discuss the matter like adults, and Theo would make her see. She had never wanted him. He had never wanted her. The only logical solution was for both of them to find a better match.

He tightened his jaw. Lady Beatrice would not understand why Theo would follow his heart rather than increase his connections. Theo's father would not understand, either.

His heart skipped. His father and Lady Beatrice would be the first in a long line of obstacles and resistance. People would talk. Theo's name would appear in the scandal columns. He would lose the one thing he'd worked his life to maintain: his impeccable reputation.

Even if the full truth of Virginia's past never came to light, her emergence as his wife would cause a firestorm. Caricatures would be just the beginning.

Theo clenched his fingers. He didn't care what people said about him anymore, as long as Virginia was by his side. She was worth everything.

The trick would be convincing her he was worth the risk, too.

"You said your London Season was unfruitful," he began, then winced. Subtle transition to the topic of marriage? Not in the least. But now that he'd begun... "Have you considered marrying in the years since?"

Virginia blanched. "I will never wed."

So, yes. She had considered. And the answer was no. Theo could not risk asking until he'd developed an argument capable of convincing her.

A feat, he realized with a suddenly heavy heart, that might be impossible. Virginia's greatest fear was being discarded. Which was, in effect, what Theo would be forced to do with his current, "perfect" intended in order to be with Virginia. The very act of choosing her over Lady Beatrice could make Virginia believe Theo would one day reject her, too.

There *had* to be a way to prove this was different. That what they shared was real and valuable.

Virginia shivered in his arms and Theo tightened his embrace. Their sleigh ride could not last forever. The sun was setting.

"To the cottage," Theo called to the footman.

The driver took the next break from the trees.

Theo's eyes widened in surprise. They were closer to the cottage than Theo had realized. He looked down at Virginia.

"Have dinner with me," he said urgently. "Not just tonight. Every day for as long as I'm here."

And every day after. Just as soon as he figured out the best way to propose.

Virginia made no such promise, but accompanied him into the cottage.

Inside the dining room, Theo paused before they took their seats.

"Here." He slid the small book of poetry from its secret home next to his heart. "You loaned me a book. Allow me to do the same."

It wasn't just a book, of course. This tiny volume was part of his soul. The part that protected him. That gave him words when he had none.

"This is..." Virginia's eyes were wide and searching.

She did understand.

Theo crossed his arms. He already felt naked without the book of poetry to protect him. Although he no longer needed to fear enemy fire, he'd never left his heart more vulnerable.

A footman strode into the dining room, bearing not a food platter but a newspaper. "Swinton says you'll want to see this."

Frowning, Theo accepted the paper.

His first fortnight in Christmas, Theo had scoured its pages eagerly, hoping for news of home. Of course there was none. No one in his family had ever comported themselves in such a manner as to cause their name to appear in a scandal column. Theo had stopped paying attention.

But there, on the front page, was Theo's own likeness. Right beneath a heading that read:

*Presumed dead.*

He sat down hard in the closest chair.

Virginia took the one beside him. "What happened?"

He pointed. "Gossip."

According to the article—if, indeed, fiction this outrageous could be considered an "article"— Major Viscount Ormondton had been mortally wounded in France. Reports that he had still been alive when removed from the battlefield could not be substantiated. His corpse had not been returned to his family, who could not properly grieve without knowing the truth.

Bollocks, all of it.

He lifted his head. "Swinton!"

The butler materialized with the portable writing desk Theo had been planning to request.

"My 'grieving' parents already know I'm alive," he told Virginia as he dragged foolscap and ink from the desk to the table. "To the rest, this twaddle will come as a shock. I'll have to ensure everyone I can think of that there is no need for mourning."

"Can I help?" Virginia asked. "I can post letters in the morning."

She was right. It was dark. Nothing could be mailed until dawn. Theo pushed the papers aside. There was plenty of time to think about the right words while he enjoyed a quiet dinner with Virginia. He turned to smile at her.

Her face had gone ashen.

His stomach tumbled in alarm. "What is it?"

"You're not the only one in the paper." Her voice shook.

"They wrote about you?" he asked in surprise.

She shook her head. "My sister."

He yanked the paper in front of him and scanned until he found the word *Underwood*.

It seemed Miss Vera Underwood, youngest daughter and the last of her siblings to marry, was now betrothed to a baron. Theo frowned in confusion.

*Last of three unwed daughters.*

"How many sisters do you have?" he asked.

"Three." Her brittle smile did not reach her eyes. "There are four of us. I guess I've been dead far longer than you."

Theo pulled her into his arms. It was time to come back alive.

# CHAPTER 11

*V*irginia had come to think of the Duke of Azureford's cottage as a second nest.

For days, Theodore had been taking extra care of her. After a whirlwind fortnight of sleigh rides, lazy afternoons, and romantic dinners, the sting of Virginia's parents writing her off as dead had begun to fade. No matter what her family wished, she was very much alive. And happier than she'd ever been back then.

Theodore was incredibly sweet and considerate. What had begun as afternoon constitutionals had turned into all day affairs lasting well past sundown. Her only complaint was that her time with him could not last forever.

His knee was about as healed as it would ever get. Once Theodore realized he would never be rid of the brace, he would also realize there was nothing else Virginia could do for him. No reason to stay in Christmas. Back home, he had people who loved him, missed him, worried about him.

He belonged elsewhere. And so did she.

She rose from the chaise longue they'd been sharing in his private parlor. "It's late. I should go."

"Wait." His fingertips brushed her arm. "I've been working up to something all week. I wanted to wait until I could do this."

He unhooked his leg brace and placed it on the floor.

Virginia watched as he rose to his feet, favoring his good leg.

She forced a smile and gestured at the discarded brace. "If you don't need that, you no longer need me. Is that what you wanted me to see?"

"The opposite." His dark gaze focused on her. "I'm trying to do this right."

He dropped to bended knee. Although Theodore could not hide a wince of pain, he did not budge from the uncomfortable position. Instead, he reached for her hand.

"Miss Virginia Underwood," he began, his voice low and warm.

"W-wait," she stammered, her words faint. "What is happening?"

"I'm proposing," he whispered. "Be quiet until I finish. This bit is nerve-wracking."

Her lungs caught. He *couldn't* be proposing. Not to her. No one wanted to keep her. Yet her pounding heart wanted so much to believe.

"Miss Virginia Underwood," he said again. He pressed a kiss to the back of her hands then placed her fingers to his chest. "Please say that you will make me the happiest of men and become my wife, for richer, for poorer, in sickness and in health, to love and to cherish, now and forevermore."

The backs of her eyes pricked. She was too lightheaded to process what this might mean.

"It was a short proposal," he whispered. "You can talk now."

Virginia doubted she could do any such thing. She was thrilled and terrified, hopeful and dumbfounded. Her heart was exploding. She'd dreaded having to continue without Theodore, but had never truly entertained the possibility of becoming his wife. This was either a dream come true or a nightmare.

"I know what you're thinking," he said. "You can't renege on the cat. If you want to see Duke again, you have to accept me, too."

A startled laugh escaped her tight throat. "I *loaned* Duke."

"Until I'm completely healed," he reminded her. "These scars are here to stay. I suspect the brace is, too. I'm sorry, darling. You fell for the oldest trick in the book."

She tilted her head. "You read books about stealing a woman's cat in order to trick her into marrying you?"

"Practical battle tactics," he assured her. "When you marry me, I'll share my library, too."

His library... in the middle of London. The one city she never wished to see again, and that definitely would not welcome her.

"I haven't agreed to anything," she stammered.

He hiccupped.

She blinked.

He hiccupped again.

"Damn it." He yanked off his cravat and placed it in front of his mouth as though to muffle the sound. "My very first proposal is the worst one in hic—history."

After another hiccup, he clamped his mouth shut tight.

Virginia recognized his fierce expression. He was reciting his favorite poem to try to make the hiccups go away.

She'd read his book. She hated that poem. There was another she liked much better. She quoted it aloud:

*"I love the moon's pure, holy light,*
*Pour'd on the calm, sequester'd stream;*
*The gale, fresh from the wings of night,*
*Which drinks the early solar beam;*

*The smile of heaven, when storms subside,*
*When the moist clouds first break away;*
*The sober tints of even-tide,*
*Ere yet forgotten by the day.*

*Such sights, such sounds, my fancy please,*
*And set my wearied spirit free:*
*And one who takes delight in these,*
*Can never fail of loving thee!"*

He stared at her in awe. "You memorized one of Miss Bethem's poems?"

"I memorized all of them." She clasped her hands to her chest. It worked! "Your hiccups are gone."

"Your selection worked faster than mine." His brown eyes shone. "I was right to give you that book."

Virginia frowned. "You loaned it to me."

"I gave it to you," he said firmly.

She shook her head. "It's an extension of your soul. You can't give away your most precious possession."

He took her hands again. "If you come with me, I can have both my favorite things."

There was nothing she wanted more than Theodore as her husband. But he hated gossip and needed to keep his reputation. To him, she would be an embarrassment and an albatross. Living like that would destroy her; would destroy *them*. It couldn't last.

"Marriage is impossible," she said, her voice small and miserable. "Surely you see that."

He tightened his hold on her hands. "You accepted me just as I am. Why can't you do the same for yourself?"

Was it possible? Did he truly see her, just as she was, and want her anyway?

"I'm hopeless in social situations," she stammered. "I don't want to anger you or hurt you or embarrass you—"

"In case it wasn't clear," Theodore said with a crooked smile, "I am, at this very moment, extremely embarrassed that my heartfelt proposal has not solicited a definitive answer, much less the 'yes' I was hoping for. If you'll promise me your hand, I won't care about the rest. I don't want to wed High Society. I want to marry *you*."

Her heart leapt. Might they be able to find some way it could work?

"We wouldn't need to go to London until you inherit?" she suggested hopefully.

He shook his head. "I have to be in London at least part of the year. But I would never force you into that world all at once. We can practice, little by little, so that you'll be comfortable when it's time."

Virginia's skin itched. "You make it sound as easy as exercising a wounded limb until it works again."

"Easy?" His brows lifted. "It'll be exactly that hard. But I managed. So have all the strays you've helped over the years. So can you."

Her chest tightened. Could she bear returning to London? This time, she would not be alone. Theodore would be by her side. So would her closest friends, who also planned to spend their Seasons in London.

She drew a shaky breath. "Do we have to attend mad crushes?"

"You don't have to do a single thing unless you wish to," Theodore promised. "Attend what you like. Stay home when you like. Speak with whom you like. Ignore whom you like." He pressed a kiss to her fingers. "As long as it isn't me. I intend to be right next to you, no matter where you are."

Her breath caught at the picture he painted.

"Just tell me what you need, and it will be yours." He set his jaw. "I'll rent Almack's on a Tuesday so that we have it all to ourselves. If there's a play you fancy, I'll purchase every seat in the theatre." His eyes twinkled. "I'll even share my private folly overlooking my favorite pond."

Despite herself, the corners of Virginia's mouth twitched. "You say that *now*."

"And I will mean it forever." He pressed her hands to his heart. "I have never broken my word, nor would I ever break wedding vows. I promise you now your home will always be with me, come what may. But only if you want me, too."

Want him? She cupped his face in her hands and kissed him with all the love in her heart.

This man was her first thought every morning; her last thought every night. The promise of having him not just in her thoughts but right there in her arms, in her bed, in her body... Her pulse skipped with desire and excitement. Home would be right here in Theodore's embrace. Her heart soared as joy flooded her. Soon, they would belong to each other.

"Wait," she gasped and forced herself to pull away.

He touched his forehead to hers. "Not until we're married?"

"Not until we're betrothed." Her stomach tightened.

He pulled back. "That wasn't a yes?"

Virginia took a deep breath. "I cannot accept

your proposal until Lady Beatrice knows she won't be receiving one."

He frowned. "She knows there's no contract. Her father schemed with mine, but I never once said—"

She stopped him. "There are all sorts of promises a person can make without saying a word."

Theodore's expression was blank. Virginia tried to make him see.

"My parents never verbally promised to love me and look out for me, but I believed it, and was destroyed when I was wrong." She shuddered at the memory. "Even if you never made Lady Beatrice an explicit promise, she believes she is your future wife, and you know she thinks so."

He rubbed the back of his neck and sighed. "You're right. Our fathers tried to plan our lives when we were children. Now that we're adults, it's time we plan our own. I will speak to her." He lifted his dark gaze. "Might you perhaps provisionally accept in the meantime?"

"I promise to give you a proper answer when you're truly free to ask."

"Then I can get up off my knee?"

"Up off your knee at once, you addlepate." She tugged him from the floor to the chaise longue.

As he fell back against the cushions, he pulled her with him and cradled her in his arms.

Virginia snuggled into Theodore and tried to calm her erratically pounding pulse. She wanted nothing more than to say yes to his proposal, to believe they had a future together, that happiness was something they could have.

The truth was, there was no way to know what the future held. Her only option was to do the one thing she had sworn never to do again: trust someone with her heart.

hen Virginia awoke, she was not tucked away in her castle guest chamber but curled against Theodore's chest. Her eyes widened. They'd fallen asleep in each other's arms.

They lay fully clothed on his chaise longue, not tangled naked in the middle of his bed, yet she could not help but suspect *those* mornings would begin much like this one. Warm and safe, her cheek nestled next to Theodore's heart. She had no interest in disturbing his slumber.

Excitement coursed through her. The past dozen hours had turned her world on its ear. Not just accidentally spending the night with a *ton* gentleman, but being proposed to. She was almost betrothed. No one would believe it. Virginia could scarce credit the miracle herself.

The moment was too wonderful. She reveled in Theodore's strength, his heat, his scent. No one at the castle would notice her failure to come home. But once she married, that would never be true again. They would start and end every day in each other's arms. She would belong.

Her chest filled with joy. She had never believed a happy ever after existed in her future, but it was starting right now. Her life with him would—

Loud bangs crashed against the knocker without cease.

Virginia winced. Someone had come looking for her. One of her friends, no doubt. How had she believed her indiscretion would go unnoticed?

She eased out of Theodore's arms and down the corridor without bothering to shake out her skirts or fix her matted hair. There was no fresh gown to change into, and besides, her friends saw each other in worse dishabille than this when they slept in one another's homes and stayed up all night. Now they would definitely have something to talk about.

Virginia came to a standstill. The woman standing just inside the entryway was not a familiar face at all.

This exquisitely dressed young lady—flanked by a pair of equally elegant lady's maids—wore a fur-trimmed pelisse, a bejeweled gold tiara atop perfect blonde ringlets, and an expression of pure contempt.

"What do you mean he is not receiving?" The woman's tone was baffled. "I've traveled for days to be reunited with my intended. Surely you don't mean to send me away without a chance to speak with him?"

Virginia's heart dropped. *Lady Beatrice.* It could be no one else.

She stepped forward.

Lady Beatrice frowned. "Who are you?"

"Miss Virginia Underwood," Virginia stammered out of reflex.

Her chest fluttered with panic. If typical *ton* interactions were difficult to navigate, this one had her completely at sixes and sevens.

"Impossible." Lady Beatrice shook her head. "I am acquainted with the Underwood girls. Their eldest sister died almost a decade ago."

Virginia did not answer. Her breath had been stolen away. There was the proof she hadn't wanted. Her family had planned on never letting her back in their lives.

Lady Beatrice's eyes widened, as though taking in every aspect of Virginia's person. The freckles that ran in the family. The same cheekbones, the same red-brown hair. There could be no doubt.

"You're alive?" she asked in confusion. "What in the world is going on? Why are you tucked away up here with—" Her cheeks flushed scarlet. "Oh. I see."

"No," Virginia said quickly. "It isn't what you think."

It was, in a way, much worse than what Lady Beatrice thought. Virginia wasn't Theodore's secret lover. He wanted her to be his wife. Or so he'd said.

If the idea of marrying Theodore had sounded like a dream come true, Lady Beatrice's presence had just awoken Virginia from her slumber. She was not the wicked witch of a fairy story, but a polite, pretty young lady who had traveled cross country to retrieve what was hers.

Not only had Lady Beatrice spent her entire life expecting to wed Theodore, she had been bred from birth to be the perfect wife, the perfect hostess, the perfect marchioness. Lady Beatrice wasn't some vague promise Theodore's father had made. She was the sort of lady a future marquess needed by his side. The exact opposite of Virginia.

Lady Beatrice wasn't just the better choice. She was the *only* choice. One look at her, and Theodore would realize how close he'd come to a terrible mistake.

"I'm sorry I tried to…" Virginia's heart was breaking too much to continue.

Even though walking away was the right path —the *inevitable* path—she hated to give up a single moment with Theodore. And yet they all knew a man like him could never choose a woman like her. She was too strange, too different, too embarrassing. It was better to leave of her own free will than to wait to be tossed aside.

Legs shaking, she stumbled around elegant Lady Beatrice and her equally elegant maids toward the door.

Lady Beatrice's gaze jerked up and her face blanched. "Ormondton, your *face*… Oh, and your leg!"

"Virginia," Theodore's voice growled. "*Wait.* I will not—"

"No." The words scratched from her throat as she spun around to face him. "It is I who will not. I cannot, and neither can you. Lady Beatrice is welcome in Society, and I am not. She belongs in your world, and I do not. *She* is your intended." Virginia swallowed the lump in her throat. "Not me."

"His…" Lady Beatrice's jaw dropped. "You were going to marry *her*? What about your reputation? What about *me*?"

"Don't worry." Virginia reached for the door. "You win."

Theodore limped forward. "I'm not a thing that can be won or lost. This isn't a game."

"Of course 'High Society' is a game," she said with a sigh. "You're both players. I am not. Marrying each other is how you win. That's why your fathers made the match. They wanted to ensure you made the right decision."

"My life is not his to run." Theodore stepped forward. "Perhaps I'll be fighting for his approval the rest of eternity, but I—"

"You're not even *in* that war." Virginia wished he could see the truth. "Your father is fighting himself. He doesn't hate you. He's just scared."

Theodore scoffed. "Scared of what?"

"Losing his worth." She curled her trembling fingers into fists. "Admitting you're ready means acknowledging his son doesn't need him anymore. Of course he's terrified. Nothing is worse than being disposable."

# CHAPTER 13

*N*othing *is worse than being disposable.*
        When Virginia's voice cracked, so did Theo's heart. His stomach roiled. Misery was etched into every inch of Virginia's face.

He reached for her. "You have never been disposable."

"I have always been disposable," she corrected with a humorless laugh. "Dreams only last until morning. I knew better than to fill my head with fantasies for this very reason. I'm not 'good *ton.*' I don't fit in. And I can never be *her.* We had our make-believe. This is good-bye."

Virginia shoved open the door and walked out.

"*Wait.*" Theo hurried down the front step, wincing at the impact on his knee. "Virginia!"

Lady Beatrice grabbed his arm. "Where are you going?"

"After her!"

Theo forced himself to stop and take a breath. Lady Beatrice was innocent. She deserved an explanation.

"I'm sorry." He turned to face her so that she could see the honesty in his eyes. "This is not what I meant to happen, or how I hoped to share the news."

"It's *true?*" Lady Beatrice's face was lined with disbelief. "You meant to throw me over for her?"

"You and I have no contract," Theo reminded her. "That is why you wrote to me for the first time, is it not? To encourage an official arrangement. I'm afraid I must disappoint you on this score. I will not be offering for your hand. Nor should you want it."

"Of course I want it." Lady Beatrice crossed her arms. "I don't mind if you keep a mistress or if we remain strangers after the wedding. I'm to be your marchioness. Combining our families is more important than personal feelings we may or may not have about the match."

"Is it?" Theo asked softly. "You should mind very much if your husband wishes to remain a stranger after the wedding. Duty is important, but not more so than love. Find a man who makes you happy, Lady Beatrice, and marry *him.*"

Lady Beatrice gestured at the narrow road winding toward the castle. "*She* is what makes you happy? What about your reputation?"

"My reputation is meaningless," he replied, "if I fail to fight for what truly matters."

For years, Theo's preoccupation with conforming to expected behavior had ruled his life. But Virginia had never been interested in marrying a future marquess. She had wanted to wed Theo, the man. From the moment they'd met, she'd accepted him exactly as he was. All she ever wanted was for him to do the same.

"What about your father?" Lady Beatrice burst out. "If you do this, he will never forgive you."

"If that's true," Theo said, "so be it."

He did not need his father's consent to decide what sort of life he wanted to live. In the choice between Virginia and the rest of Society... Theo chose Virginia.

"*Swinton*," he called.

Swinton materialized at once. "Yes, Mr. T?"

Happiness was right up that hill. "Please summon my coach."

"The sleigh is blocking the way, sir." A ghost of a smile touched the edges of the butler's mouth. "And it would be faster."

"Fine," Theo growled. "Ready the sleigh."

"The *what?*" Lady Beatrice's brows shot up. "Where do you think you're going?"

"To beg for Virginia's hand." Theo rolled back his shoulders as the sleigh pulled into sight. "Go home to London."

"But she doesn't even want you anymore," Lady Beatrice stammered. "She said this was goodbye!"

Theo would change Virginia's mind or die trying.

"It *is* goodbye," he said as he climbed into the sleigh. "To fear, to each other, and to our parents' manipulations. Live for yourself, Lady Beatrice. Choose happiness. It's the only decision worth making."

# CHAPTER 14

*V*irginia wrapped her arms about her chest and huddled into the wind as she climbed the final stretch toward the castle.

Her throat felt swollen. The bitter wind blowing through her heart came not from the air around her, but from having come face-to-face with the sort of woman Theodore's father expected him to marry. Nothing less than perfection would do.

Lady Beatrice was everything Virginia had imagined her to be. Beautiful, composed, wealthy, popular, more than comfortable in her role as a lady. The ideal marchioness. She would never cause embarrassment.

Virginia's eyes pricked with heat. By trying to force herself where she did not belong, Virginia would only make Theodore's life harder... just as she'd done to her own family.

'Twas better to cut things off now, before greater damage could occur. If Virginia's parents had rid themselves of her in order to have a normal life, what did she expect from Theodore?

"Miss Underwood!"

Virginia glanced up in surprise. Although she was still several yards from the castle's entrance, the solicitor had all but burst from the open doors as if he had been desperately awaiting her arrival.

"The aviary," he panted upon reaching her side, "is a resounding success."

Virginia did not congratulate him. It would be a long time before she felt like celebrating anything. She had hoped to trudge up the seventy-two steps to her guest chamber without speaking to anyone at all.

"It's chaos," the solicitor continued, eyes wide. "Every guest in the castle crammed elbow-to-elbow inside a four thousand square foot box."

"Four thousand, six hundred and eight," Virginia muttered. "The aviary is an oval."

The solicitor increased his pace to keep up. "No one knows it better than you."

"You hired an expert," she reminded him without pausing. "A man."

"And he's wonderful," the solicitor assured her. "But the new veterinarian is only one man. There is simply too much work for a single person, no matter how much expert experience they might have."

Virginia pushed through the castle doors.

The solicitor continued on her heels. "Please think it over."

"Think what over?" She crossed toward the stairs. "You haven't imparted new information."

He cut in front of her. "The veterinarian occasionally needs to sleep. I realize you dislike crowds, but could you not pop by from time to time when visiting hours are over to ensure all is well? And possibly once or twice during the day, so he might take a bite to eat?"

Virginia shook her head. "You realize I dislike crowds. You just said so."

"I know." The solicitor held out his hands in supplication. "What I forgot to mention is that I am not asking you for a favor. I'm offering a permanent position. If you agree to co-manage the aviary, your salary will equal the new veterinarian's."

She halted in shock. The solicitor was acknowledging her value. Wished her to stay on permanently. Was willing to pay her the same as a *man*.

"What do you say?" he asked. "Are you the woman for the job?"

Virginia spun away from the stairs and turned toward the aviary instead.

The solicitor beamed at her as he hurried to keep step. "Is that a yes?"

"I don't know," she answered honestly.

Managing the aviary wasn't one of the futures she had imagined. As much as Virginia adored the castle and loved Christmas, she wasn't even certain she could withstand the limited interactions required to run a private animal sanatorium. Presiding over four thousand, six hundred and eight feet of pure chaos sounded like a nightmare.

Yet, they needed her. *Wanted* her. How could

she say no? Mr. Marlowe had taken Virginia in and shown compassion at a time when all hope was gone. This was an opportunity to pay back that kindness.

"Please say yes," the solicitor begged. "You're irreplaceable."

*Irreplaceable.*

Virginia's head swam. She had dreamed of being necessary to someone, anyone. But that was only one part. She'd hoped to build a life on her own terms, not accept yet another role someone else thrust upon her.

"I'll consider it," she said. It was the least she could do.

"Thank you." Just as they reached the aviary, the solicitor placed a hand on her arm. "Before I take my leave… A letter arrived for you."

She stared at him. "A letter?"

In the six years Virginia had lived in Christmas, in the three years she'd been locked in an asylum, in the eighteen years from birth to her disastrous London come-out, Virginia had never once received a letter.

She accepted the document with shaking hands.

The solicitor bowed and headed off to grant her privacy.

Virginia broke the seal. Her mouth fell open as the contents became clear.

This wasn't personal correspondence. This was notification of a bank draft deposited in her name. The fund manager wished to assure her that the astronomical sum mentioned covered her portion of perfume royalties for the partial month since the debut of *Duke* and *Duchess* collectible turtle-dove bottles. All further remittances would cover a full month's payment.

Virginia pressed the document to her chest and tried to breathe. Her pulse raced at the implications.

For the first time in her life, she was not only a woman of independent means, but a person with *options*.

She could stay right here. This castle, this aviary, this village.

Or she could go elsewhere. Use this money to establish her animal sanatorium anywhere she pleased. The Highlands, the beach, the Cotswolds. Anything she pleased.

Her future was truly up to her.

Giddy excitement filled her chest. She could not wait to tell Theodore. He—

Would not be part of her future.

The happiness fell from her face. They would never share joyful news again. She tried to push the heartbreak from her mind.

This was not the first time she'd lost someone she loved. She would have to be strong and make her own path. Starting with her promise to consider the aviary.

She opened the door and froze just inside the threshold.

The solicitor had not exaggerated. In London, the *haut ton* wouldn't even be awake at this hour, yet the castle guests had filled the aviary almost to capacity.

Not just guests, Virginia realized as she forced herself to inch deeper into the loud, bustling crowd. There was Angelica Parker, the town jeweler. Over there were all three le Duc siblings. Far in the back were Gloria and her betrothed, Christopher. Virginia steadied her nerves.

If she wanted to survive this crowd, she needed a friend. Virginia made her way in their direction, keeping her eyes firmly on the ground before her.

"What are you doing here?" Gloria whispered when Virginia reached her side. "Didn't you notice all the people?"

Virginia nodded. She hadn't just noticed all the people. She'd *traversed* them. Taken one hundred and sixty steps from the aviary entrance to where her friends stood on the other side, despite the deafening noise, despite the wayward elbows, despite the onslaught of clashing scents and colors. Her spine straightened.

If she could emerge victorious when faced with such a gauntlet, she could certainly open a private animal sanatorium.

This village was too comforting to leave and too limiting to stay. She would be forever grateful to Mr. Marlowe for taking her in when she had nowhere else to go, but she would not spend the next fifty years in a guest chamber. Christmas had healed her when she was wounded and needed shelter, but now that she was healed, Virginia could not allow it to become a gilded cage.

"Don't look now," Gloria whispered. "*Lord Ormondton* just walked through the door."

Virginia could not possibly look. Every muscle had frozen in place.

"I thought you said Ormondton was at war," Gloria whispered to her betrothed.

"He looks like he's been at war," Christopher murmured back. "What the devil is he doing *here?*"

Gasps rustled through the crowd.

Virginia did not move.

"Miss Virginia Underwood," a familiar, gravelly voice boomed from the other side of the aviary. "This is not goodbye. I cannot leave whilst you still possess my heart."

"Holy Christmas." Gloria melted against her intended's chest. "This is absolutely making the papers."

*Scandal columns?* Theodore would not take such a risk.

Slowly, Virginia turned around.

Hundreds of wide-eyed onlookers fell back against each other, creating a narrow chasm between Virginia's section of the aviary and the main entrance directly opposite, where Theodore stood. Her heart flipped.

He had not paused to change clothes.

His dark hair was awry. His fine jacket was bunched at odd angles. His absent neckcloth was wherever he'd dropped it after his hiccups the night before. His scarred face was unbandaged. His wounded leg was encased in a stiff metal brace.

He had never looked more dashing.

"Wouldn't it be easier to marry someone else?" Virginia called out, her voice shaking.

"*Marriage?*" Gloria kicked Virginia's shin. "Lord Ormondton wants to make you his wife, and you fail to mention that tiny detail to your bosom friend?"

"It's complicated," Virginia whispered back. "And mostly my cat's fault."

"I'm not looking for easy," Theodore answered, his voice ringing clear. "I'm looking for you."

Her pulse skipped.

"I don't want temporary," he called out. "Life won't be worth living if it means leaving you behind. I want forever. I want *you.*"

She caught her breath.

"You're as necessary to me as breathing." He pressed a hand to his heart. "You make me whole."

Her heart pounded.

"I love you," he called out. "I'm here to prove it."

Excited whispers rolled through the crowd like the crashing waves of the sea.

Theodore took one limping step closer. "I, Theodore O'Hanlon, Major Viscount Ormondton, want you, Miss Virginia Underwood…"

"I'm swooning," Gloria whispered. "I can't watch because my heart is exploding."

"To be my wife," Theodore continued, striding forward as if his damaged limb was not screaming with pain. "From this day forward; for better, for worse…"

Gloria kicked Virginia's other shin. "Go to him, you ninny!"

"For richer, for poorer…" Theodore took another uneven step.

Virginia summoned her courage and started through the crowd. "In sickness and in health…"

Theodore began to walk faster. "To love and to cherish…"

"Until death do us part." Virginia ran the rest of the way until they stood less than a breath apart.

With a crooked smile, he took her hands in his. "Is that a yes?"

"I love you," Virginia blurted, and lifted her lips to his.

"It's a yes!" Gloria called out.

The crowd erupted into deafening shouts.

Virginia barely flinched at the noise. Her heart was too full. "Is your carriage close by?"

"My sleigh." His cheeks colored. "I may have left in a hurry."

"Sleighs are splendid." She turned toward the door and linked her fingers through his.

Whatever the future held, they would face it together.

# CHAPTER 15

*London, England*
*Two months later*

$\mathcal{V}$irginia gripped Theodore's hand and tried to pretend her stomach wasn't overflowing with butterflies. Although they had arrived at his town house last month after their wedding, tonight would be Virginia's first official public outing.

"It won't be small," Theodore warned as their carriage inched along the queue. "Not as crowded as Almack's, but a respectable soirée all the same. We don't have to do this if you're not ready."

"It's the last major gathering of the Season," she reminded him. "I want you to dance with your cousin."

The heat in his gaze could have melted choco-late. "I want to dance with *you.*"

Virginia's hands went clammy. Dancing in the privacy of their home was one thing. Here, hun-dreds of eyes would be upon her.

Their carriage came to a stop. A footman opened the door. They were here.

"Ready?" Theodore asked.

Virginia was not ready. She was terrified. But with Theodore at her side, she knew she could brave anything.

He handed her out of the carriage and led her to the front door.

When the butler greeted them, Theodore handed him a calling card Virginia had never seen.

"What is *that?*" she asked, unable to stifle a giggle.

"Four colly birds," he answered with a straight face. "And a cat. I didn't want Duke to feel he wasn't part of the family. You know how he likes to meet new people."

"You didn't bring him, did you?" she asked in mock horror.

"No one *brings* Duke." Theodore widened his eyes innocently. "If there's an open window, Duke will find us."

The butler beckoned. "This way, if you please."

Limbs shaking, Virginia pressed her elbows into her sides and forced her stiff legs to follow.

When the butler announced them at the head of a small ballroom, all eyes swiveled their way, exactly as she had feared.

To her surprise, Virginia recognized several friendly faces. There was Noelle and her husband, the Duke of Silkridge. Penelope and her husband Nicholas. Even Gloria, and her husband Christopher. Virginia's tight muscles relaxed.

A soirée no longer felt like enemy territory, but a haven stocked with friends.

"I see my cousin," Theodore murmured. "She's trying to blend with the wainscoting."

"Go dance," Virginia said without hesitation. Hester had dined with them several times and was a truly lovely young lady. She would be thrilled.

Theodore shook his head. "I don't want to leave you without—"

"Virginia!" All three of her closest friends squealed as they surrounded her with smiles and excited hugs. "You made it!"

Virginia grinned. She *had* made it. In every sense. She was happily married to a wonderful husband. She was back in London, and thriving despite her fears. She was even here at a Society soirée, reunited with her friends.

"Go," she told Theodore with a smile. "Find me after your dance with Hester."

She could not be prouder of him.

Theodore had made it, too, in all the ways that mattered. He'd survived war, then his homecoming. His peers were thrilled to have him home again. His brace and scars were seen as marks of bravery, not folly. The only gossip in the papers were the laments of eligible debutantes, vexed that the dashing viscount had fallen in love in his absence.

"Virginia?" came a shaky voice right behind her.

Her smile froze. Virginia would recognize that voice anywhere. It sounded just like her own. She turned on stiff legs. The night had only wanted this.

Before her stood three young ladies with red-brown hair and hesitant green eyes. Virginia's sisters.

"Valeria," she said evenly. "Vera. Viveca."

Vera, the youngest, threw her arms about Virginia. "I missed you so much!"

Viveca and Valeria talked over each other in excitement. "Mother said—"

"Father insisted—"

"We thought you were dead!"

"It was horrible to lose a sister." Vera's eyes shone with tears. "The worst pain you can imagine."

"When we saw the papers—"

"The announcement that Lord Ormondton was back, and marrying *you*—"

"It was the miracle we'd never dreamed to hope for!" they said at once.

Vera threw her arms around Virginia. "Please say you'll have us back. We love you so much."

Virginia's throat was too tight to release all the words trapped in her heart. "But… what about Mother and Father?"

Her sisters' faces fell.

"I'm sorry," Viveca said softly. "A fever took them several years back."

Virginia braced herself for the pain of loss. It didn't come.

Instead, something closer to relief swept over her. Her family hadn't ignored and forgotten her all these years. The only two people who knew where she was, were gone. To her sisters, Virginia hadn't been inconsequential at all. If they'd had any notion, they'd have come to her at once.

"We would love to be family again," Valeria said with a shy smile.

The music changed, and Vera's face lit up. "It's a quadrille! Perfect for four couples."

"*Do* say you'll join us." Valeria squeezed Virginia's hand. "I can think of nothing better than sharing the last soirée of the Season with every one of my sisters."

Virginia could think of nothing better than starting the rest of her life reunited with her family.

Theodore appeared at her side. "Am I interrupting something?"

"You're just in time." She grinned at her sisters and took a deep breath. "We're going to dance a quadrille."

His eyebrows shot up and he proffered his arm at once. "Who do I thank for this miracle?"

"Valeria, Vera, and Viveca." Virginia's happy smile wobbled as she gazed at them. "I just realized I cannot make proper introductions because I don't know all your new names."

"I can't wait to tell you everything that's happened," Vera gushed. "I've been keeping a list—"

"It's not a list," Viveca interrupted. "From the day you died, she began all her diary entries with 'Dear Virginia.'"

"How do you know?" Vera demanded.

Valeria and Viveca exchanged innocent glances.

"You two are the worst." Vera looped her arm through Virginia's free side. "Don't be friends with them. They don't deserve you."

"Did you really write me letters?" Virginia asked in wonder.

Vera nodded. "Every night. They won't admit it, but they did, too." She gave Virginia a mischievous smile. "I peeked."

"Come along," Viveca called. "We're missing the start of the quadrille!"

As Virginia and Theodore took their places, she squeezed his hands.

"I love you," she whispered. "Without you, none of this would have happened."

"I believe you have that backward." He gestured at his knee brace, then the ballroom around them. "None of this would have happened without *you*, Lady Ormondton. You tamed my heart and complete my soul."

# EPILOGUE

*One year later*

Searching for Virginia, Theo dashed up one side of the folly overlooking the family pond with a basket dangling under one arm. Just as he reached the top, her head rose from the other side.

"The heart has only four chambers, but its capacity to love is infinite." She grinned at him. "Looking for me?"

He answered by taking her mouth in a kiss.

"I brought you something," he murmured.

"So did I." Her eyes sparkled. "You first."

He set the basket on the wide balustrade and began unloading small, frost-covered dishes.

She burst out laughing. "Ice cream?"

"Start with the chocolate," he suggested, and handed her a spoon.

Virginia dipped the spoon into the dish and frowned. "Remind me to talk to the chef. Parts of this are frozen solid. It feels like—"

Her head jerked up toward his, eyes round.

He blinked back at her innocently.

"There's a key in my ice cream." She dug through the dish to retrieve her prize. "Why is there a key in my ice cream?"

He lifted his shoulders.

With a squeal, she set down the dish and launched herself into his arms. "We got the property?"

"*You* have the property." He held her tight. "The one you wanted, halfway between here and Christmas. Now you'll never be more than a few hours away from one of your many animal sanatoriums."

"Many?" She pulled away with a laugh. "First there was one, and now there's two."

"That's how the aviary started," he replied with a straight face. "Go ask Dancer how many birds there are now."

Virginia spun around in joy. "This is everything I dreamed! The London sanatorium can concentrate on pets and strays, and our new country location can specialize in wildlife."

"Be sure to save a few hours in your busy day for me," he growled as he pulled her back into his arms.

"Nights," she corrected wickedly. "I promised you my nights."

He wiggled his brows. "At least I was clever enough not to promise there'd be time to sleep."

Sighing happily, she rested her cheek on his chest and snuggled close. "Did you ever think we would have all this?"

Theo pressed a kiss to the top of her head.

Every aspect of their life together was a dream come true. They'd carved a place in Society. His wife was brilliant with animals. Marlowe Castle had employed a second veterinarian, but was always thrilled when Virginia stopped by the aviary.

They divided their time between London, Christmas, and the marquessate's country pile. Father was finally allowing Theo to take part in a few projects. He and the marquess weren't quite bosom friends, but they were slowly learning how to work side-by-side. It was more than Theo had dared to hope.

Virginia lifted her head from Theo's chest and hesitated. "When we were at the Duke of Azureford's cottage—"

A black ball of fur streaked up the folly steps, hissed at them both, then disappeared into the basket of ice cream.

Theo sighed. So much for their treats. He grinned at Virginia. "When we were at Azureford's?"

Her cheeks turned pink and she nodded. "You once said you found me… poetic."

"I *always* find you poetic." He touched her cheek. "You have a gift, my love. You should write down some of your—"

She reached into her reticule and handed him a small book.

His mouth fell open.

"You published your poetry?" He thumbed through the pages in awe. His wife was the most talented, capable woman he knew. "This is marvelous. I cannot wait to tell everyone I know."

"There's only one copy," she said in a rush, then bit her lip. "I thought you might like it."

"I love it." He swept her into his arms. "And I love *you*."

For the rest of his life, he would keep her poems tucked next to his heart.

THE END

~

**When the Duke of Azureford finally returns to his holiday cottage, he *and* his heart are in for a surprise!**

Join the fun in *Dukes, Actually*, the next romance in the *12 Dukes of Christmas* series!

# AUTHOR'S NOTE

*T*oday, we have words like "on the spectrum" and "high functioning" to explain why Virginia experiences the world differently than others.

The Regency Era, when this story takes place, is one hundred years before the first use of the word "autism," and even further removed from the resources and growing understanding that we have today.

Virginia's parents would have had no frame of reference for why their child was not behaving as they wished. It would likewise be impossible for Virginia to fulfill their desires.

Finding friends, safety, and agency in a town like Christmas would have been a godsend for Virginia.

Here, she can interact as much as she wishes and seek privacy and less stimulation whenever she needs, allowing her to explore the world on her terms and at her pace, and finally realize she is every bit as smart, talented, and worthy as everyone else. She has a place. She is wanted. She belongs.

Someone as wonderful as Virginia doesn't just deserve love. She deserves happily ever after.

As for Theo? The poor man never had a chance. ;-)

xoxo,

Erica

THANK YOU FOR READING

**Love talking books with fellow readers?**

Join the *Historical Romance Book Club* for prizes, books, and live chats with your favorite romance authors:
　　Facebook.com/groups/HistRomBookClub

Check out the *12 Dukes of Christmas* facebook group for giveaways and exclusive content:
　　Facebook.com/groups/DukesOfChristmas

Join the *Rogues to Riches* facebook group for insider info and first looks at future books in the series:
　　Facebook.com/groups/RoguesToRiches

Check out the *Dukes of War* facebook group for giveaways and exclusive content:
　　Facebook.com/groups/DukesOfWar

And check out the official website for sneak peeks and more:

www.EricaRidley.com/books

# ACKNOWLEDGMENTS

As always, I could not have written this book without the invaluable support of my critique partner, beta readers, and copy editor. Huge thanks go out to Erica Monroe, Jennifer Connor, Tracy Emro, and Nikki Groom. You are the best!

Lastly, I want to thank the *12 Dukes of Christmas* facebook group, my *Historical Romance Book Club,* and my fabulous street team. Your enthusiasm makes the romance happen.

Thank you so much!

# ABOUT THE AUTHOR

Erica Ridley is a *New York Times* and *USA Today* best-selling author of historical romance novels.

In the new *Rogues to Riches* historical romance series, Cinderella stories aren't just for princesses… Sigh-worthy Regency rogues sweep strong-willed young ladies into whirlwind rags-to-riches romance with rollicking adventure.

The popular *Dukes of War* series features roguish peers and dashing war heroes who return from battle only to be thrust into the splendor and madness of Regency England.

When not reading or writing romances, Erica can be found riding camels in Africa, zip-lining through rainforests in Central America, or getting hopelessly lost in the middle of Budapest.

~

*Let's be friends! Find Erica on:*
www.EricaRidley.com